ENTHUSIASTIC PRAISE FOR BLACKJACK!

"*Blackjack* is a quick, entertaining read. Feld's knowledge of the equine is apparent on each page; detailed descriptions of the movements and responses of the horses bring the reader right into the world of these splendid animals. This book will keep horse lovers reading well beyond lights out."

— *ForeWord Magazine*

"Mrs. Feld has a true gift in capturing the imagination and engaging the reader. It isn't always easy to find a set of books that will be read willingly by pre-teens! Kudos to Mrs. Feld on her delightful *Morgan Horse* series."

— Jenefer Igarashi, Senior Editor,
The Old Schoolhouse Magazine

"Ellen Feld has a knack for writing for young readers, and the first book in her *Morgan Horse* series, *Blackjack*, is sure to entertain horse-loving kids. Young riders will understand the bond that Heather Richardson has with her much-loved Morgan, Blackjack, and will be rooting for her as she tries to rescue the jet-black stallion from an abusive trainer. Feld's entertaining *Morgan Horse* series is a perfect way to encourage young riders to become enthusiastic young readers!"

— Lesley Ward, Editor,
Young Rider Magazine

"*Blackjack* is packed with information about the care and training of horses. The reader will experience the thrill of competition in the ring as Heather and·Blackjack participate in shows. The story is well-constructed with an exciting plot and interesting characters. Anyone who loves horses will love this series."

— *Catholic Library Journal*

"A wonderful story about the special bond between a girl and her horse. There is something in this book for everyone who likes horses."

> — Brian Sosby, Editor,
> *Equestrian Magazine*

"Feld takes the reader through a whirlwind of emotions in *Blackjack*. Her accurate and detailed descriptions of basic horsemanship and stable management make the *Morgan Horse* series books not only fun adventure stories, but educational as well."

> — Susan Dudasik,
> *Just Horses Magazine*

"Younger girls will be inspired ... adult girls will remember back to when just being near a horse was all you needed to make your day."

> — Katherine Walcott,
> *Eventing USA*

"It is nice to read a junior novel that focuses on a teenager and a Morgan Horse. Ellen Feld has written a warm and rewarding horse story. This book would make a great present for a young rider and reader."

> — *Horsemen's Yankee Pedlar*

"*Blackjack* is a fast-reading, enchanting story about a girl and a Morgan Horse. The book will greatly appeal to readers as there is plenty of horse action, starting in the first chapter. Author Ellen Feld has written a lovely story about the exceptional love between a girl and a beautiful, majestic horse."

> — Anthony Locorini, Editor,
> *TriState Horse*

BLACKJACK:

Dreaming of a Morgan Horse

THE MORGAN HORSE SERIES
BY ELLEN F. FELD
Read Them All!

Blackjack: Dreaming of a Morgan Horse

ISBN 978-0-9709002-8-9

An International Reading Association— Children's Book Council "Children's Choices" Selection

"Mrs. Feld has a true gift in capturing the imagination and engaging the reader. It isn't always easy to find a book that will be read willingly by pre-teens! Kudos to Mrs. Feld on her delightful *Morgan Horse* series."

— Jenefer Igarashi, Senior Editor, *The Old Schoolhouse Magazine*

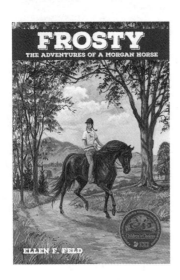

Frosty: The Adventures of a Morgan Horse

ISBN 978-0-9831138-6-7

An International Reading Association— Children's Book Council "Children's Choices" Selection

"... a thoroughly delightful novel for young readers about a girl and her relationship with powerful and noble animals ... Frosty is a story to be cherished by horse lovers of all ages."

—*Midwest Book Review*

Rusty: The High-Flying Morgan Horse

ISBN 978-0-9831138-2-9

A Parent to Parent Adding Wisdom Award Winner

"Through her choice words and obvious first-hand knowledge, Ellen Feld conveys to the reader that special connection a girl has with her horse. A thoroughly enjoyable read—I only wish it had been published when I was a teenager!"

—Cindy Mark, Editor, *Horses All*

Robin: The Lovable Morgan Horse

ISBN 978-0-9709002-5-8

A Parent to Parent Adding Wisdom Award Winner

"Feld uses plenty of conflict on many levels, a string of obstacles, and the characters' solutions to craft a very interesting story with a quick pace. We rated this book five hearts."

—Bob Spear, *Heartland Reviews*

Annie: The Mysterious Morgan Horse

ISBN 978-0-9709002-9-6

A Moonbeam Children's Book Award Winner and A Reader Views Literary Award Winner

"Annie combines an exciting story with a lot of practical information. It's another blue-ribbon winner from author Ellen Feld!"

—*Horsemen's Yankee Pedlar*

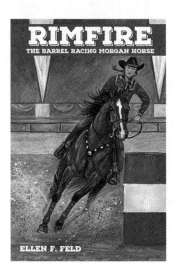

Rimfire: The Barrel Racing Morgan Horse

ISBN 978-0-9709002-1-0

Selected as the Best New Book for 2010 by Tack 'n Togs Magazine

"Rimfire brings the exciting world of barrel racing to life in a fun and delightful way! A great book for our youth and a valuable reminder that quitters never win and winners never quit."

—Martha Josey, *AQHA, WPRA,*
NBHA World Champion,
Olympic Medalist, Hall of Fame

Blackjack: The Champion Morgan Horse

ISBN 978-1-7337674-2-2

This book "... has excitement, suspense, and a surprise ending, all coming together with a satisfying understanding of horses. It is another blue-ribbon winner from a talented author."

—Nancy Norton, Editor,
  Horse & Academy Magazine

Meet the Morgans

ISBN 978-1-7337674-3-9

The perfect companion book to the popular *Morgan Horse* series. With over 50 photos of the real horses behind the books, readers will get an inside look at the Morgans who inspired the series.

ALSO FROM WILLOW BEND PUBLISHING

Blackjack: The Magical Morgan Horse

ISBN: 978-0-9831138-6-7

A girl, a horse, and some magical stardust - sometimes dreams really do come true...

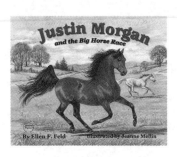

Justin Morgan and the Big Horse Race

ISBN 978-0-9831138-1-2

"A beautiful story with magnificent drawings that's pure entertainment."

—Amy Lignor, *Feathered Quill Book Reviews*

Shadow: The Curious Morgan Horse

ISBN 978-0-9831138-3-6

A USA Book News Best Books Award Winner

"You are guaranteed to delight in this story of a young, adventurous foal. Feld is a talented, creative, artistic writer who clearly loves her topic of horses. Absolutely delightful!"

—Viviane Crystal, *Crystal Reviews*

Pidgy's Surprise

ISBN 978-0-9831138-0-5

"Written and fantastically illustrated by famed equine artist Jeanne Mellin, this re-release of a popular story from the 1950's offers a heart-felt story of a young girl and her discovery of the path of her dreams."

— *BookPleasures.com*

What Can I Do?
A Donkey-Donk Story

ISBN: 978-0-9831138-7-4

"If you are searching for a picture book to read to your homeschooler or class that will illicit smiles, peels of laughter, and giggles, then look no further."

— *Valerie Schuetta, M.Ed.,*
  Classroom Reviews

Horse Show!
A Donkey-Donk Story

ISBN: 978-1-7337674-0-8

"A joyful gigglefest that also teaches a valuable lesson. Young readers will love Donkey-Donk's adventure."

— Holly Connors, *Feathered Quill*
  Book Reviews

Take A Hike!
A Donkey-Donk Story

ISBN: 978-1-7337674-1-5

Follow Donkey-Donk as she hikes to the top of Mount Washington and enjoy the incredible scenery that she discovers.

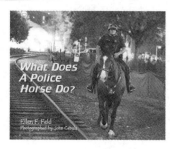

What Does A Police Horse Do?

ISBN 978-0-9831138-9-8

Meet Liam - a police horse with the Lancaster, PA Mounted Police Unit. Follow along with this very special horse to learn just what a police horse does every day.

BLACKJACK:

Dreaming of a Morgan Horse

Ellen F. Feld

Willow Bend Publishing
Goshen, Massachusetts

Illustrated by Jeanne Mellin
Cover design by 8 Create Graphic Design
Book design by Linda Mahoney, LM Design
Composition by Susan Leonard

Library of Congress Catalog Card Number: 2001116635
ISBN: 978-0-9709002-8-9

Direct inquiries to:
Willow Bend Publishing
P.O. Box 304
Goshen, MA 01032
www.willowbendpublishing.com

Printed in the United States of America

10   9   8   7

To Dad

*for always putting up
with my horse endeavors,
no matter how silly,
with a smile on his face.*

ACKNOWLEDGMENTS

I would like to thank Dr. Mary M. Shaw for the medical consultation, Carrie White-Parrish at Eleven & Company for her meticulous review of this story as well as Jacquelyn Tolksdorf of 8 Create Graphic Design for her cover graphics. In addition, I would like to thank Jeanne Mellin for the beautiful artwork she created for this book.

THE ALARM

She knew she had to hurry. It would be light in just a few hours, and then somebody might see her. The air was crisp, stars were everywhere and a full moon filled the sky. There were no streetlights on this road ... and without the moonlight, she'd be lost.

Suddenly there was something coming at her; she squinted her eyes to see better. Headlights! *Hurry, hide.* She quickly jumped down into a ditch at the side of the road. There was no time to look and see what evil night creatures might be hiding down there, and—yuck—there was something wet and slimy under her. It felt like a giant slug, or maybe it was a night crawler, those big slippery worms that often came out after rainstorms.

She put her head down and covered it with her hands. When the car approached, the wheels made crunching sounds as they rolled over the gravel on the road. Slowly peering up over the ditch, she saw the car pass. Once it was gone, the only sound was that of crickets, chirping loudly.

"Wow, I never knew crickets made so much noise," she whispered to herself. Getting up, she climbed up from the ditch, spit grass and dirt out of her mouth, and rubbed her shirt and jeans with her hands. On her shirt were the slimy remnants of whatever it was that had jumped aboard. She wiped her hands on the dew-laden grass and continued the journey.

Ahead of her, the road curved slowly, and once it eventually straightened out again, a house became visible. Finally! Off in the distance a dog barked. Hopefully, it was very far away. She turned her attention to the house. It was huge, about four times the size of her parents' home. There appeared to be three floors, and the exterior was all brick except for the wooden shingles, which were painted white. What was it like to live in such an enormous house? With everything you could possibly want? What—*Come on now, you're wasting precious time, gotta keep going, hurry up, hurry up,* she interrupted herself firmly.

Moving on, she wandered across the wet grass toward the barn. Like the house, the barn was huge. She had heard it had 40 stalls, and after seeing the outside, there was no doubt that it easily had that many, maybe even more. It was made of beautiful wood, probably cedar. None of that inexpensive aluminum siding here; this barn was built by people who had a lot of money and wanted the world to know. High above the main door, the name "Three Forks Farm" was proudly displayed in brightly painted red letters. At the end of the word "Farm," a silhouette of a magnificent black horse pranced.

The door itself was actually made of two sliding sections, large enough to allow easy passage of a horse and cart.

She approached and cautiously tried to open one side. It slid about an inch and stopped, so she tried the other side. It also slid about an inch and stopped. It must have been locked from the inside. How would she get in?

Please hurry, hurry and find a way in. You're wasting time!

Maybe there was a way in through the back. She began to walk around to the right of the barn, and as she got close to the corner she noticed that there was another section of the barn that had not been visible before. No, wait a minute, that wasn't another section of the barn; it was an indoor arena, which was attached to the side of the barn. It too was huge. Everything at this place seemed to be. All of a sudden, a dog began barking.

Oh no, hurry, hurry!

At the edge of the arena, she found a door. She grasped the doorknob but was afraid to try to open it. Most big barns like this had fancy security systems installed to keep away people like her. The last thing she wanted to do was set off such a device. But with no other way to get in, she decided to try and open it. Surprisingly, the doorknob turned and clicked, and the door opened. Her eyes grew wide, like a young child surprised by a new puppy.

Once inside, she was immediately met with the sweet smell of freshly cut hay. Unable to see in the dark building, she pulled a small flashlight from her pocket and quickly scanned the arena with the light it provided. This was a gorgeous building, with paneled walls and a very high ceiling. She turned toward the barn, and as she did so, the corner of her right eye caught a glimpse of something—or some-one. She tried to scream, but no sound came out of her mouth. Turning to run, she managed to trip over her own feet and tumbled to the ground in what would have been described as a belly flop if anyone had been around to see it. But there was no one, for as she got up, terrified, looking in the direction of the evil ghoul, she realized that the side of the arena was covered with mirrors. The "someone" she had seen was her own image reflected in the mirror.

Boy, did she feel foolish.

Once again brushing dirt off her shirt and jeans, she looked around to get her bearings. There was a wall between the arena and barn, which had a large sliding door, but unlike the outside doors, this one was wide open. She quickly passed through it.

Entering the barn, she heard the sounds of several horses munching hay, and every once in a while a horse would sneeze. There was a faint light coming from the ceiling. Perhaps a groom did barn checks late at night and needed a light kept on. This light, along with her flashlight, allowed her to see pretty well. Looking down the aisle, she saw stalls, lots of them.

With such a big barn, how was she ever going to find Blackjack?

She walked over to the first stall and was able to easily look inside, since the doors only went halfway up, but couldn't see a thing. As she raised her arm so that her flashlight could give her a hint of what lay inside, something lunged at her. She jerked her body backward just in time to avoid the extremely sharp teeth of a very unpleasant horse. Just as quickly as it had appeared, the horse disappeared. The girl took a cautious step forward and the horse lunged at her again. This time, though, it kept its head outside the stall, ears flat back, showing its teeth.

This was not going to work. How would she ever find her horse and get him out of here before daylight? Suddenly, an idea popped into her head. She could whistle to him. It had always worked in the pasture. He'd be out with the other horses, far off in the distance. So far in fact that she was unable to make out which horse was hers. She would call out with her special whistle and Blackjack would immediately pick up his head, prick his ears forward, and listen. He would never respond until she whistled a second time. Then he'd whinny loudly and come galloping through the field toward her. His eagerness almost always got the other horses excited, too, and they'd follow him through the pasture to the barn. Once at the barn (it was built inside the pasture), Blackjack would go zooming past her, do a sliding stop just in time to avoid hitting the fence, and then turn and rear at the same time. As his feet hit the ground after rearing, his wild stallion routine would end and he'd become the big baby he truly was.

There was no way she would ever find him in here if she had to search each stall, so she decided to give the whistle a try. But when she whistled, no one answered. She tried again, this time a little louder. Immediately, there was a loud, deep whinny. It was coming from the far end of the barn. She turned toward the whinny and started walking ... and then running. The horse whinnied again. She quickly reached the stall and found Blackjack sticking his head out, trying to reach her, too. As she approached him, she dropped her flashlight, oblivious to it now that her beloved horse was found. Flinging her arms up and wrapping them around his big, black neck, she allowed his full Morgan mane to cover her face and hide the tears that streamed from her eyes.

"I found you, I found you," she kept whispering softly to him. Blackjack turned his head so that he could see her. His jet-black coat glistened, even in this limited light, and the half-moon star on his forehead was a welcome sight. He nuzzled her gently. She smiled slightly and kissed him on the nose. "I've got to get you out of here."

Quick, quick, she had to hurry. She found a halter and lead rope hanging on the outside of his stall door, grabbed them, and returned to her horse. She reached up to his head and slid the halter on. Normally he would nip playfully at the halter, but

he seemed to sense the urgency, and behaved perfectly. Together the horse and the girl left the stall. But as she led Blackjack down the aisle, the other horses started to whinny, perhaps expecting to be fed. They got louder and louder until it seemed likely the owners in the great big house could hear. She had to get out of there quickly.

She led Blackjack toward the main entrance, where the big sliding doors were. She tried to slide one of them open, but just like the first time, when she was trying to get in, it moved an inch or so and then stopped. The lock on the floor was keeping the door from opening. Without thinking, she bent down and unlatched it.

Instantly, a loud, blaring alarm went off.

"Oh no, we're caught! It's the alarm, the alarm, the alarm!"

"Come on Heather, wake up, you're going to be late for school! Can't you hear your alarm?"

A New Bus Driver

Heather jumped up with astonishing speed, whacked the alarm clock, and then fell back to bed just as quickly. She had perfected this move over the years and had become so accomplished at it that she could perform it with her eyes shut and easily fall back to sleep afterwards.

With the alarm clock silenced, she lay in bed, not moving a muscle. She was trying to open her eyes but they seemed to be glued shut. Finally, with a quiet groan, she managed to open them. As her mind slowly drifted to consciousness, she realized that today was the start of the spring semester at school. *Oh yuck*, she thought, *I've got to take Industrial Design this semester.*

She groaned again, rolled over on her back, and then threw the thick, warm comforter over her head, hoping that she could somehow hide from the world.

With her head buried beneath the comforter, Heather remembered the dream that had once again been interrupted. This was the third time she had had the mysterious vision about the beautiful black Morgan. It always ended the same; with the barn alarm going off and Heather waking to the blaring sound of her own alarm clock. Perhaps it was an omen of things to come.

Yeah, right, thought Heather, *my life could never be that exciting.*

Her mind wandered to thoughts of her riding the handsome black horse through rolling fields of tall grass, and she started drifting back to sleep.

Suddenly the comforter was violently pulled away from her head.

"Heather, come on, didn't you hear me?! You're going to be late for school. Come on, get going!" With that, her mother pulled the comforter off the bed.

"Geeze, Mom, I'm freezing and I'm so tired. Can't I sleep just a little longer?" pleaded Heather. Hearing no answer, she turned her head slowly in the direction of her mother's voice. There she saw her mom, hand on hip, long brown hair neatly brushed, eyes looking down at her. She didn't seem very happy. They exchanged glances and Heather knew by the look in her mom's eyes that she had better get moving.

How did her mom do it? It was only a little after 7 a.m. but she was already dressed, and by the smell drifting into her room, had also had time to make a hearty breakfast for her daughter.

With a loud groan, Heather dragged herself out of bed and proceeded, ever so slowly, toward the bathroom. Out of the corner of her eye, she saw her mother watching her. Like the alarm clock tactic, this too had become part of Heather's morning ritual. Her mom wouldn't leave until she knew Heather was in the shower.

Dressed in jeans and a pretty white blouse, with sparkling blue eyes, Heather's mom always seemed to be smiling. Everyone told Heather she had inherited her good looks from her mother, and, like her, Heather had bright blue eyes, and a long mane of deep brown hair. Unlike her mother, however, Heather never wore her hair loose. Instead, she always kept it in two tight braids with brightly colored elastics at the end of each one. Her friends had tried unsuccessfully to convince her to start wearing her hair loose. She was, after all, fifteen years old; in fact she'd be sixteen in just a few months. But Heather wasn't interested in dressing up; she preferred to be comfortable, and so ignored the requests of her friends. She also preferred dressing in blue jeans like her mom, although she favored t-shirts over blouses.

By the time Heather had showered and gotten dressed it was already 7:20—and the school bus would be arriving at any moment.

"Mom!" she hollered as she ran by the kitchen. "I don't have time to eat! I've gotta go!"

When she got outside, the frigid air hit her hard. "Ugh, I hate winter!" she mumbled to herself. She

11

quickly put on her thick winter jacket and zipped it up to her chin. In an attempt to stay warm, she raised her shoulders and sunk her head down into the jacket.

When Heather reached the end of her short driveway, she saw the school bus approaching her stop, and immediately broke into a full sprint, knowing she'd have to hurry to make it. The stop was five houses away, and even though the bus went right by her house, the cranky old bus driver refused to stop anywhere but at the designated place. Heather arrived just as the bus door opened. Driving the bus was not the usual cranky woman, but rather a kindly old man, slightly bent over from age and with an abundant amount of gray hair.

"Welcome aboard, young lady. Have a seat and warm up."

Heather slowly climbed into the bus. The first seat behind the driver was free and, not having the energy to walk any further, she sat down. The bus was wonderfully warm, and as it sped off to its next stop, Heather struck up a conversation with the driver.

"What happened to our regular driver?"

"She decided it was time for a more relaxing job, so she took the place of somebody in the office who was retiring," replied the amiable man.

"Oh, that's nice, I guess. She was always a nasty old lady, yelling at us all the time, so I won't miss her. By the way, my name is Heather."

"I'm Chauncy, pleased to meet you."

Heather could see Chauncy's weathered face in the rearview mirror, and clearly saw a huge smile. *This is a driver I'm going to like,* she thought.

The rest of the ride to school passed quickly as she and Chauncy continued their friendly conversation. By the time they arrived at school, Heather had completely warmed up, which made the frozen arctic air that greeted her as she exited the bus even harder to take.

"It's been nice talking to you, Chauncy. Have a great day."

"You too, Heather."

With that, Heather made her way out of the bus and into school, which was abuzz with activity. Everyone seemed excited at the thought of new classes. Most people were talking more loudly than usual and the locker doors seemed noisier when slammed shut. As Heather walked to her locker, she had to maneuver through large groups of people who were too busy laughing and shouting to notice her. Arriving at her locker, she opened it and reached in for the math book she had used last semester—she would need it for this semester's math class too.

The school day passed quickly, and then it was time for the last class of the day, Industrial Design. Now that sounded like a class to sleep through.

Heather sat on a high stool and leaned on her desk, listening to the teacher. Their desks in this class were architectural desks—which could be adjusted to different angles. *Great*, she thought, *I can find just the right position to take a good nap*. The teacher, Mr. Robinson, had a very dull, monotone voice. How was she ever going to get through this class?

The first lesson consisted of Mr. Robinson talking about how wonderful his course was for forty-five long, dull minutes. Most of the other students looked just as bored as Heather, and she wondered how many of them really wanted to be in this class.

"So as you can see," Mr. Robinson continued, "Industrial Design is a very exciting field that has a lot of applications in the real world. I see that we are almost out of time, but before we go, I'd like to give you your first assignment."

Ugh, thought Heather, *homework already*. Several students groaned.

"It won't be that bad," encouraged Mr. Robinson. "I'd like you all to start thinking of what sort of a building you would like to design. By Friday, I want you to hand in a one-page proposal."

With that, the bell rang and it was time to go home. Everyone seemed happy that the first day of the new semester was over.

Heather waited for the bus alone. All of her friends took different buses, which stopped further up along the sidewalk. When her bus finally came, she climbed on last and was glad to see that the first seat was still available. She preferred sitting there since it meant she could be the first one off the bus when it arrived at her stop.

"Well hello, young lady. How was your first day back at school?" asked the driver.

Heather looked up and saw Chauncy. "Oh, hi. I guess it was okay. It was good to see my friends."

"What classes are you taking?"

Heather proceeded to tell him all about her new classes as the bus drove away. When she got to her last class of the day, Industrial Design, she told him about the assignment.

"I can't believe the teacher gave us homework already. But I've been thinking about it and I have decided to propose designing a horse barn."

"I didn't know you liked horses."

"Oh, I love horses. I took riding lessons for a few years and really enjoyed them. I want to be a horse trainer someday."

"Well, I have a small horse farm. Maybe you can get your parents to bring you over to meet my Morgans."

Heather's eyes opened widely. "Did you say Morgans? I love them. They're my favorite breed!"

"Yup, I've got fourteen Morgans. A stallion, one gelding, eight mares, and four yearlings."

"Oh, I'd love to meet them! Maybe this weekend?" Heather asked, the excitement in her voice obvious.

"Sure, Saturday sounds good to me."

Chauncy had Heather write down his phone number so that her parents could call him to get directions, as well as decide on a good time to meet.

"Too bad it's only Monday; I don't think I can wait till Saturday. Hey, why are you stopping?" asked Heather.

"It's your stop."

"Oh." Heather felt pretty foolish. She jumped up and got off the bus. "Okay, see ya tomorrow," she said as she got off the bus.

MEETING THE MORGANS

"**M**om! Mom! Guess what?! Guess what?!" Heather shouted as she stormed into the kitchen.

Mrs. Richardson turned away from the sink, where she had been peeling potatoes for dinner, to look at Heather. "Slow down, honey."

"But I've got to tell you what just happened," Heather gasped as she attempted to catch her breath. She had run all the way from the bus stop to her house, eager to tell her mother the exciting news.

"Okay, I'll bite. What just happened?"

"Well, we got a new bus driver and—"

"That certainly is exciting news," interrupted Heather's mom, a bit sarcastically.

"Mom, come on. Let me finish," pleaded Heather.

"Okay, honey, I'm sorry."

"Anyway," continued Heather, "we got this new bus driver today. A really cool guy named Chauncy. We started talking on the way to school this morning and he's really nice. On the way home, he asked me about my classes. So I told him about all of them. When I got to my last class, Industrial Design, I told him that we have to design a building and I was thinking of designing a barn. He asked me why I'd want to do that so I told him about how I love horses so much and guess what?" Before Mrs. Richardson had a chance to respond, Heather answered for her. "He has a small horse farm and he's invited us to come visit this weekend! Isn't that great, Mom? Can you believe it?"

"But Heather, we don't know anything about this Chauncy. I'm not going to let you go running off to some stranger's place."

"But Mom," Heather interrupted again. "He doesn't want just me to come visit, he wants *all* of us! He gave me his phone number so you can call him. He said he'd be around on Saturday. Please, Mom, can we go?"

"Well, I don't know, honey. Let me talk to Dad when he gets home tonight."

"But what's there to talk about? It's just to go out to a farm and look at some horses. Please?" Heather looked at her mother with pleading eyes.

"I promise I'll talk to him tonight."

"Thanks. Here's his phone number." Heather reached into the front pocket of her jeans and pulled out a crinkled piece of paper. She handed it to her mom and then headed down the hall toward her room.

That night, Heather had trouble falling asleep because she was so excited about the prospect of going to a real horse farm. Unfortunately, her dad didn't get home until very late. As her parents talked, Heather tried to figure out what they were saying, but the noise of the television drowned out the conversation, and all she could hear was mumbling. That was the last thing she remembered before falling asleep.

The following morning, Heather was wide-awake before her alarm went off. She lay in bed for a while, thinking about all the beautiful horses that might live at Chauncy's farm. Perhaps he had a gorgeous black stallion, like the one in her dreams. But Morgans were typically bay, so the chances of finding a black stallion were unlikely. But what else might she find? A pretty little bay mare, with a long, flowing mane and tail, or perhaps a tall, lanky chestnut gelding with four white socks and a star on his forehead? Now that sounded nice. Maybe Chauncy would even let her ride one of his horses. With a smile on her face, Heather slowly stretched her whole body and got out of bed. She stuck her head out of her room and could smell the aroma of bacon cooking.

"So did you call him?" Heather asked as she sat down for breakfast.

"What, honey? Oh, you mean Chauncy? No I didn't call him. By the time your dad got home, it was too late."

"But Dad said it was okay?" questioned Heather.

"Yup, your dad thought it sounded like fun. So I'll call Mr., um, what is his last name?"

"Gee, Mom, you know, I forgot to ask."

Heather managed to eat all of her breakfast, have a nice talk about school with her mom, and still leave the house with plenty of time to catch the bus. Getting up early sure had its advantages, although sleeping late was definitely more enjoyable. When the bus finally arrived, Heather was fifth in line to get on. She wanted to tell Chauncy what her mother had said about visiting his farm, but when she got on the bus she was disappointed to find the first three seats behind him already taken. She smiled at him and then continued down the aisle until she found an unoccupied seat about halfway down.

Before long, the bus pulled into the schoolyard and came to a screeching halt. Instantly, everyone got up and crowded into the aisle. As the last person slowly walked past her, Heather got up and walked toward Chauncy.

"Hi there."

Chauncy turned to face the voice. "Oh, hi Heather."

"I just wanted to let you know that my mom said she'd call you today. She said Saturday would be good and that even my Dad will come."

"Okay. I'll be home most of the day and will look forward to her call."

"Great! See ya." Heather turned away from him and stepped down off the bus.

The day went by quickly, and even Industrial Design seemed interesting. Heather had told the teacher about her plan to design a barn, and to her surprise, Mr. Robinson liked the idea.

"I think that's great, Heather. You could design something really unique."

"It'll be fun," she replied. "I just met someone who has a horse farm, so I'm going to ask him what he would put in an ideal barn."

With that, Heather headed out the door. She stopped at her locker long enough to get her jacket and toss her notebook and pencil into the mess that had become her second home, then put her jacket on and headed out the door. The line for her bus was already long, and she knew that she'd never get the front seat. She stood at the end of the line and listened to the babbling of the two girls in front of her. They were arguing about which girl in their English class had been the worst dressed that day.

21

Fortunately, the bus came quickly, and she was not subjected to too much of their nonsense.

When she got on the bus, she smiled at Chauncy.

"Your mom called me today, Heather. We're all set for Saturday at 10 o'clock."

She stopped and turned to face him while people pushed past her, some grumbling at her for being in the way.

"Great! I can't wait!"

The rest of the week dragged by as Heather's anticipation of Saturday increased day by day. Finally, the long-awaited weekend arrived. The day dawned bright and chilly. The high was expected to be 35 degrees, which was considered pretty warm for early February. Still, it was very cold for visiting a horse farm. Heather was up, showered, and dressed by 8:30.

"Hi, Mom, hi, Dad," she greeted her parents as she entered the kitchen. Mr. Richardson was already sitting down, reading the paper and drinking his coffee. Her father was a handsome man, in his mid-forties and about six feet tall, with a full head of black hair. As soon as he heard Heather, he looked up and acknowledged her.

"Hi, kiddo, how are ya?"

"I'm great, Dad. I can't wait to go to Chauncy's farm. I've been looking forward to it all week."

"That's what your mom tells me. I'm looking forward to it, too. It should be a lot of fun, although I expect the barn is going to be awfully cold."

"Heather, do you want bacon or sausage with your eggs?"

"Sausage, Mom."

The rest of the meal was filled with small talk, mostly about what was going on at school. Finally, breakfast was over and the Richardson family headed off to Chauncy's farm.

"My directions say that the farm is on the left hand side, about one and a half miles down Mill Creek Road, so we should be seeing it shortly," said Mrs. Richardson, as she looked at her directions for the umpteenth time.

"There it is, there it is!" shouted Heather, pointing to a barn off in the distance.

"That looks like it," agreed Mr. Richardson. He drove slowly as he approached the barn, peering out the window to look for a house. The barn was set back a bit from the road, and was slightly hidden by several tall maple trees growing near it.

They pulled into the driveway next to the sign advertising "Gallant Morgans for Fun and Families."

Although Mill Creek Road was in sorry shape, the driveway appeared to have been paved within the last year. The car followed the driveway as it went up a slight hill and then curved around the maple trees until the house came into view. The ranch-style house was painted barn red. *How appropriate,* Heather thought.

Her dad turned off the engine and all three of them sighed at the same time as they climbed out of the car and the cold air hit them. They walked toward the front door, not saying a word. The only sound was the crunching of the snow under their feet. As they approached the door, it opened and Chauncy's smiling face appeared.

"Well, hello there, everyone. I'm glad you could make it."

"How could we miss such an opportunity?" responded Mrs. Richardson. "Heather has been talking about this all week. Hi, I'm Heather's mom, Mrs. Richardson. We talked on the phone." She held out her hand.

Chauncy reached out to shake hands and then said, "Please come in. It's far too cold outside."

Heather and her mom entered the house, followed by Mr. Richardson. Instantly the wonderful aroma of freshly baked bread met them.

"You must be Mr. Richardson," Chauncy said.

"Yes, it's a pleasure to meet you, Mr. Campbell," Heather's dad replied as he walked into the living room. It was tastefully decorated with a brown sofa along one wall facing two large, comfortable-looking recliners on the other. A lovely brass model of a prancing horse was proudly displayed in the middle of the room on a small oak coffee table. At the far end of the room was a fireplace, and on the mantel above sat several silver pewter trophies, no doubt won by Mr. Campbell's horses. In one of the far corners, the one between the sofa and the fireplace, a television sat on a low stand.

"Would anyone like some hot chocolate?" came a voice from another room. Everyone turned to see a slightly plump woman with an enormous smile enter the room. She wore a pastel blue dress with slightly puffy shoulders, her short, silver-gray hair brushed back away from her face. She had a very gentle appearance, and spoke softly.

"Hi there, I'm Mrs. Campbell. It's a pleasure to meet you all. You must be Heather. I've heard all about your plans for the special barn that you are designing in school."

Heather began to blush. She couldn't believe that Chauncy had actually bothered to mention her project to his wife.

"Yes, I'm Heather. It's so nice to meet you. I'm so excited about being here and getting a chance to meet some horses."

"But before you see the animals, please come into the kitchen to warm up with hot chocolate. I've also got some raisin bread that I just baked."

They slowly made their way into the kitchen. It, too, was nicely decorated with simple but functional furniture, a gas stove, a plain white refrigerator, and an extra deep sink, the sort often found in old New England farmhouses. There was a counter that separated the cooking area from the eating area, and walking around it, Heather and the others all reached for the steaming cups of hot chocolate that Mrs. Campbell had placed there. Heather carried her cup over to the table and sat down. Like the living room, the kitchen also had a mantel at the far end. But unlike the other mantel, this one was covered with numerous photos of young children. Heather sat there and examined the pictures.

As Mrs. Campbell brought the bread, butter, and plates over to the table, she noticed Heather's interest in the photos. "Those are our five children," she said proudly. "They're all grown up now, and we're expecting our first grandchild in a few months!"

"You have lovely children," Mrs. Richardson politely replied, noticing the photos for the first time. In several of the photos, the children were riding horses either through a pasture or at a horse show.

As her parents and the Campbells continued with their talk about families, Heather turned to glance out of the large bay window behind her. To her surprise and joy, she saw several horses romping in the snow.

"Oh, wow! They're gorgeous!" she exclaimed.

Everyone turned in Heather's direction.

"Would you like to go meet them now?" asked Chauncy.

"Yeah, I'd love to!" replied Heather.

"I think I'll stay in the house, dear. It is a bit too cold out for me today," said Mrs. Campbell. "Would you like to stay in with me, Mrs. Richardson?"

"Call me Helen, and yes, I would. Why don't you go out with Heather, dear," Mrs. Richardson suggested as she looked at her husband.

"Okay, let's go," Heather's dad said with a smile.

"Oh, gosh, what I would give to have a barn like this in my backyard!" sighed Heather as they made their way down a narrow path to the barn, a short distance away. Her dad and Chauncy just smiled.

From the outside, the barn appeared to be very simple. The bottom half was made of cinder block and the upper half was wood, painted barn red. There was a single large, sliding door at the front, where they stopped. Chauncy reached over to the door handle and, with a grunt, opened the large door. As soon as the horses heard the rumble of the sliding door, several of them nickered.

The wonderful smell of hay caught Heather's attention first. Then she looked down the main aisle in awe. The barn certainly wasn't fancy, but it was clean and neat. Just like the outside, the inside was built with cinder block going halfway up the stalls with the upper half made of oak. Each stall had a simple wooden door, and on each door was a hook upon which hung a halter and lead rope. There were no top sections to the doors, which allowed the horses to hang their heads out so they could watch all that was going on in the barn. There were five stalls on each side and what appeared to be a tack room next to the entrance. Several horses were sticking their heads out of their stalls, each begging for attention.

"Come on. I'll introduce you," said Chauncy. "This is Gallant Queen, one of my favorites," he said as they approached the first stall. Gallant Queen was a beautiful bay mare with a full, wavy mane of black hair. She had her head and as much of her neck out of the stall as possible, straining against the door to try to get closer to Chauncy, all the while bobbing her head up and down as if to say yes. Heather giggled in delight.

"She wants a treat," explained Chauncy. He reached into his pocket and pulled out a mint. "Here, Heather. Give this to her. Just remember to keep your hand flat. That way she can't nibble your fingers by mistake."

Heather took the mint and, with great concentration, flattened her hand and reached over to Gallant Queen. The mare turned her attention to Heather's hand and gently took the mint from her.

"It tickles!" laughed Heather.

Gallant Queen began to toss her head again, looking for another mint.

"Is she begging for more?"

"Yes," answered Chauncy. "There's nothing Queen likes better than a mint."

"May I give her another one?" asked Heather.

"Just one more," replied Chauncy as he reached into his pocket and pulled out another mint. The crinkling of the wrapper caught Queen's attention and she nickered to show her excitement.

Heather gave the horse the mint and within a few seconds Queen was tossing her head again.

"No, no. No more for you, missy," Chauncy said to the mare, the affection in his voice obvious. "This here is Gallant Queen's daughter, Gallant Lady, another favorite of mine," Chauncy explained as he walked to the next stall.

This second stall contained a carbon copy of the first horse.

"She looks just like her mom," said Heather, a bit confused at the amazing similarity between the two.

"That's not unusual for well-bred Morgans, Heather. Queen has all the qualities I like in a good Morgan, and I wanted to duplicate that. Sometimes you can and sometimes you can't. I was lucky."

Heather and her dad had been standing next to Lady's stall, with their backs toward the horse, intently listening to Chauncy's explanation. Lady apparently did not like the fact that everyone was ignoring her, and so pushed Heather with her nose so hard that Heather had to take a step forward and brace herself against her dad to avoid falling.

"Hey, what do you think you're doing?" she asked jokingly as she turned around to face Lady. The horse hadn't hurt Heather, but had definitely taken her by surprise.

"She doesn't like being ignored!" chuckled Chauncy.

"Can I have another mint?" asked Heather.

"Actually, she doesn't like mints. Here give it a try, you'll see."

Chauncy handed her a mint, which Heather carefully fed to Lady, remembering to keep her hand flat. Lady took the mint and swung her head up and down several times as her teeth chomped in rhythm with her head movements. Then she spit the mint out.

"That's quite a production, Lady. It was just a little mint," said Mr. Richardson as he reached over to pet the horse on the neck. Lady snorted in agreement and leaned over to Heather, who was still standing next to her. She proceeded to rub her head on Heather's jacket, trying to find just the right spot to itch.

"You don't have to let her do that," said Chauncy. "Just say 'no' in a commanding voice."

"No," Heather said as firmly as she could. But Lady ignored her and continued scratching. "No," repeated Heather.

Lady stopped scratching and just looked at this new person. Heather was sure she saw disappointment in the horse's face.

"Oh, go ahead, I don't really mind," the girl said gently, giving in to the horse's imaginary pleas. She reached up and patted Lady on the neck. The horse began rubbing her head on her new friend again.

"She's wonderful, Chauncy. How old is she?"

"She's five years old and her mom is twelve. All of my horses have wonderful personalities and are also a lot of fun to ride, although I think Queen prefers to drive."

Before Heather realized what she was saying, she blurted out, "Oh gosh, I'd love to ride one of your horses!"

"Well I think that could be arranged, but we'll have to wait until it warms up a bit. It's too cold and icy right now."

"Okay, Chauncy, but I'm going to hold you to that. I've never ridden a Morgan before, just grade horses. I've heard Morgans are very smooth and have a great trot, so I'd like to see for myself if that is really true."

"I'm sure they will prove to you that Morgans are great riding horses, and also make fantastic best friends. They could use the exercise, too. I just drive my horses. My kids were the ones who rode them, but they can't get home very often now. Now let me show you the rest of the horses before we get too cold out here."

Chauncy walked along to the third stall. "In here somewhere is Gallant Image."

There was no horse sticking its head out of the stall, so Chauncy called the horse. "Immie, come here boy. We've got company."

A horse snorted in acknowledgment, and Heather could hear him slowly walking toward the front of the stall. Then she saw him—Blackjack!

THE DREAM HORSE

Heather could not believe what she was seeing. Standing in front of her was the horse of her dreams, the one whom she was always trying to save, the one she had to get out of the barn before the alarm went off. How could her dream horse be a real horse? She just stood there, dumbfounded, not saying a word.

The horse came to the front of the stall and stood there proudly, a bit aloof, as if to say, "Look at me!" He was the most stunning animal that Heather had ever seen. He was large for a Morgan, probably around 15.2 hands, and all black, except for a small half-moon tuft of white hair on his forehead. He had an extremely long forelock, reaching halfway down his muzzle, and soft, kind eyes that would melt any heart. Even with all his winter fuzz, Heather could tell this was a special horse.

"Chauncy," Heather exclaimed, "he's gorgeous! What did you say his name is?"

"It's Gallant Image. He's named after his dad, whose name was Imagine That. Imagine That was a world champion stallion in the in-hand and open park saddle divisions five years ago. His owner was a very good friend of mine and I was able to breed Queen to Imagine That the following spring. Unfortunately, the stallion died shortly after and only left three foals, including Immie here. So that makes Immie pretty special—and he knows it."

During Chauncy's explanation, Immie stood quietly, never moving a muscle, and Heather was unable to take her eyes off him.

"How old is he?" she asked.

"He just turned three last week. He's still growing and a bit gawky right now, but he's really going to be beautiful when he fills out."

"A bit gawky?" Heather asked, peering into the stall to look at the rest of the horse. "Where?"

"Oh, his rump is a bit high right now. But once the rest of his body catches up with his back end, he'll be fine. Look how up-headed he is!" exclaimed Chauncy, obviously very proud of his horse.

"Chauncy," interrupted Mr. Richardson, "he doesn't seem as playful as the other two we just looked at. He seems, well, a bit standoffish."

"That's because he's a stallion. He wants you to think he is something special. Would you like me to take him out for you and set him up?"

"Oh yeah, that'd be great," replied Heather in an instant.

"What does 'set up' mean?" asked Mr. Richardson.

"That means put him in a show pose," Heather answered before Chauncy could reply.

Chauncy reached for the halter that was hanging on the stall door. Seeing it, the horse lowered his head so that Chauncy could put it on him. As Chauncy slid the halter on, Immie tried to nibble at the noseband.

"Oh Immie, now stop that!" reprimanded Chauncy.

The halter was bright purple—a bit tacky, thought Heather until she saw it on the horse. The purple really made the black of his coat stand out. Chauncy took a cotton lead, also purple, and attached it to the halter.

"Excuse me, Heather," he said as he moved to open the stall door.

Heather and her dad carefully got out of the way as the door swung open. This was after all a stallion, and you always had to be very careful around them; they were so unpredictable. The door opened and Gallant Image slowly stepped out of the stall, following his owner to the middle of the aisle. Heather and her dad leaned up against the barn wall, right near Lady. The mare, hanging her head out of her stall, had been intently watching all the excitement. Immie just ignored them, his attention on Chauncy and what his owner wanted him to do.

"Okay, boy, set up," Chauncy commanded, raising his hand to be level with the horse's muzzle.

The stallion instantly moved his front legs forward just a bit and raised his neck up even more than before. Again he stood perfectly still. He seemed to know that these strangers were looking him over, checking out every inch of his body, and he intended to show them how perfect he was. Heather slowly walked along the side of the horse while her dad moved closer to Lady so that he could pet her muzzle again. As Heather walked along, studying Immie's conformation, she glanced at his head and caught his eye moving back a bit so that he could see her better. Chauncy was right; this horse was really up-headed. He had a well-angled shoulder and his neck seemed to come straight out of it. His neck was not as thick as most of the studs Heather had seen, but she expected that was because he was still young. It was obvious Immie enjoyed a lot of grooming, since his coat glistened even in the middle of the winter. *What a handsome horse,* she thought. As she reached his hind end, Immie could no longer see her, and so he turned his head slightly.

"He likes you," observed Chauncy.

"How can you tell?" she asked.

"Because normally when I show him to people, he completely ignores them. But he's keeping his eye on you; he wants to know what you're up to."

"Well then, Immie, the feeling is mutual, because I really like you too," Heather affectionately told the horse. "Has he ever been to a horse show?" she asked, turning her attention to Chauncy.

*He seemed to know that these strangers were
looking him over.*

"He will be showing in the Futurity at the big Morgan show in June," Chauncy proudly announced.

"A Futurity? What's that? A horse show?" inquired Heather.

"Actually, a Futurity is a series of special classes held over several years. The winning horses accumulate points in each class until, in the third year, the points are tallied and an overall winner is announced."

"Wow!" exclaimed Heather. "That sounds pretty neat. Immie is three, right?" She looked at Chauncy for confirmation and he nodded his head. "So how has he done so far?"

"He's done great! As a weanling he won his in-hand class, which was wonderful, especially since there were 22 horses in it! As a yearling he took second place in a really tough class. Last year, he started going through a growth spurt shortly before the show and his rump got a bit too high. He actually looked pretty gawky. So he only got a fourth place in the in-hand class, but he won the driving class. Now it looks like the rest of his body is starting to catch up with his rump, and with any luck, he might just win that in-hand class again. He'll also go in the driving class, but probably not the saddle class. I don't think we'll have him going well enough by June."

By this time Heather had walked back up to the front of Immie. She took her gloves off and began to stroke his neck, wanting to feel his soft hair without the bulky gloves coming between them. Immie responded by lowering his head. The proud stallion who had towered above her now seemed like a docile little puppy, begging for attention. He nuzzled her jacket gently as though he were looking for something.

"What's he doing?" she asked, a bit surprised by this sudden outpouring of playfulness.

"Oh, he's looking for a treat."

Chauncy handed her a mint and when she held out her hand, Immie's muzzle went right for it. The horse quickly ate the mint and then nuzzled her again, looking for more treats.

"Come on, Immie, time to go back to your stall before you forget all your manners!" scolded Chauncy as he led the magnificent stallion back to his stall and removed his halter.

The stud quietly walked back into his stall and lowered his head as he sauntered to the back of his home. He sniffed a flake of hay that had been trampled on and then, with a bit of indifference, nibbled at it. Heather peered into the stall to get one last look at her dream horse. As soon as the stallion realized he was being watched, he looked up at his new friend and then turned and walked toward her. He reached over the stall door and once again nuzzled gently at her jacket.

"You're a good boy, Immie," she murmured as she gave him a final pat on his thick, well-muscled neck.

Reluctantly, she turned her attention away from the stallion so that she could meet the rest of the Morgans.

"Let's see, who else do we have here?" Chauncy thought out loud.

"Where are the other horses?" asked Heather, looking around. "You said you had fourteen horses, but there are only ten stalls here, and it looks like a bunch of them are empty."

"I like to turn the horses out to pasture as much as possible. Let them stretch their legs, so to speak. You saw the horses from the kitchen window. Those were the yearlings. They stay outside in the big back pasture year round."

He walked over to another stall, directly across from Immie's. "Hey, Rusty, what are you doing? There's someone here who would like to meet you."

Heather approached the stall and saw a handsome bay horse quietly munching on some hay.

"This is Gallant Rusty, my all-time favorite. He's a fabulous horse and we've been through an awful lot together."

"Is he a stallion too?" asked Mr. Richardson.

"Oh no, he's a gelding. He's my driving horse, and we've really cleaned up at the open shows. My daughter has also shown him under saddle, and was very successful. Basically he's done it all. He loves to drive and also goes saddle seat, hunt, and western."

"These two here are also mother and daughter, like Queen and Lady," Chauncy explained as he approached the stall next to Rusty's. "This mare is pretty special. Her bloodlines are a mix of the real old-time horses, and such breeding is awfully hard to find nowadays. She's got Flyhawk and Dyberry Bob up close. She's not exactly a spring chicken, she'll be 21 this year, but she's still a good, sound breeding animal, and her foals are priceless."

A chestnut mare with a large white blaze walked to the front of the stall. Mr. Richardson walked right up to her, and the mare obviously appreciated the attention because she immediately started to nuzzle his neck.

"Hey, that tickles," giggled Mr. Richardson. "What's her name, Chauncy?" he asked as he gently pushed the mare's head away.

"Her registered name is Misty Meadow, but we call her Missy."

Mr. Richardson peered into the stall to get a good look at the horse. "Don't you think she could use a diet, Chauncy?" he asked. "She looks awfully plump."

"She's going to go on a major diet in early May," replied Chauncy.

Heather and her dad just looked at Chauncy. He smiled, realizing that they didn't understand.

"She's going to have a foal in May!"

"Oh..." replied Heather and her dad in unison.

"All of my broodmares are in foal," Chauncy continued. "In order to pay the bills, every horse here, with the exception of Rusty, has to earn their keep. Rusty is still used by my children when they come to visit. But the other horses must help keep the farm going."

Chauncy turned his attention to the last horse on the tour.

"This young lady is Missy's daughter, Gallant Mist. We call her Nugget." The three of them walked to the last stall where a smaller version of Missy was waiting for them. The only noticeable difference between the two horses was that the daughter did not have a blaze.

"Well, honey, I don't know about you but I'm cold," announced Mr. Richardson. "I think this has been wonderful, but I don't think we should expect Mr. Campbell to stay out here all day and freeze just so that we can enjoy his beautiful horses."

"I don't mind, but I think another mug of hot chocolate sounds good right now," replied Chauncy.

They turned and walked back toward the house, and once they were inside, Heather's mother greeted her, eager to hear of the horses they had just visited.

"Ah, Mom, they were great. They are all so friendly. And there's this one horse, a stallion. He's the most beautiful horse I've ever seen. Chauncy took him out of his stall and he just stood there like a statue. He was incredible."

"They are really something, hon," agreed Mr. Richardson. "You know I'm not a horse person, but these horses are really special. They are all so friendly, not a mean one among them."

Heather glanced out the big window overlooking the pasture, trying to see the yearlings. Suddenly, a huge gust of wind blew some of the drifting snow into the window. Instantly, from the left, four bay horses appeared. They came charging past the window, kicking their heels up at each other and at imaginary snow monsters, and bounded off through a large snowdrift, one of them stumbling as he pounded into it. The horse quickly recovered, kicked out to the right side with both legs so violently that the hind end of his body twisted and he almost stumbled again. He instantaneously regained his balance and galloped off with the rest of the horses.

Chauncy could see the longing in Heather's eyes. He had seen that look in his own children's faces when they were younger, and knew what it meant. It was obvious that she adored horses, and he wanted to give that passion a chance to develop. He had been thinking about hiring a stable hand since his youngest daughter, Laura, had moved away last fall. He could really use the help, and besides, it would give him more time to work with Immie and get him ready for the Futurity.

"Heather?" he asked.

"Yeah, Chauncy?" replied Heather, taking her attention away from the window.

"I've been thinking of getting someone to help me around the barn and I was wondering, with your parents' approval of course, if you might be interested."

"Oh, gosh, I'd love to!" exclaimed Heather, not giving him a chance to finish.

"Let me finish, Heather, because you may not be interested. I'm not just looking for someone to ride. You'd be expected to do some of the less glamorous chores like mucking stalls, sweeping the aisle, cleaning water buckets, and such. I'd also need you to give all the broodmares a good brushing and lots of attention. In exchange for this, you could ride Rusty and, once you gain some experience, start helping me with the youngsters. You could begin by coming on Saturdays and then, if things work out, maybe by spring you could come weekdays, after school. Talk to your parents and let me know next week, okay?"

"Okay Chauncy, but I know what my answer is going to be!" Heather replied excitedly. She looked at her parents, both of whom seemed to be smiling. *A good sign*, thought Heather. She would have to work on them tonight.

That evening at dinner, the conversation quickly turned to the events of the day.

"Well, what do you think, John? Should we let Heather work with Chauncy?" asked Mrs. Richardson.

"Well, dear, I don't know. What do you think?"

"Come on, guys, this is really important to me!" pleaded Heather.

"How is this going to affect your school work? I know you're a very bright girl, but you haven't been working as hard as you could lately. We can't let playing with horses get in the way of school," explained her mom.

"Your mother is right, you know. School has to come first."

"I promise that it will. I'll work twice as hard. I promise, really!" beseeched their daughter.

"Well..." started her dad, trying to drag it out for effect. "I suppose we could give it a try. But if your grades suffer, the minute they do, you'll have to give up your barn job. Is it a deal?"

"Yes, Dad! My grades will be fine, you'll see! I'm so excited. This is going to be great!"

Once she had her horse, the girl led the animal toward the side door, the one she had entered through. They approached it and the girl cautiously opened it all the way. The horse looked at the door, a bit bewildered that he should be expected to go through such a thing.

"Come on boy, you can do it," she encouraged. The horse, placing all of its trust in the girl, warily proceeded. And he did manage to get out, rubbing the right side of his hind end on the frame of the door as he passed. Once outside, she placed the lead rope around the horse's neck, and climbed onto his back. Guided only by the moonlight, they quietly made their way to the road in front of the barn and proceeded, without notice, past the house. She asked the horse to go faster and faster; it didn't matter if they stumbled in the dark, because she knew that they were safe now. Soon the horse was going at a brisk canter, his long mane flowing behind him while the girl easily sat bareback, rocking to his gentle motion. All that mattered was that she and Blackjack were free.

"We're free, Immie, we're free!" she hollered.

Heather opened her eyes. No alarm blaring in her ear, just the smell of ham frying. Now she *knew* that Immie was Blackjack!

GETTING ACQUAINTED

Monday morning dawned bright and warm. The temperature was expected to reach a high of 40 degrees, balmy for New England in February. The extended forecast called for nice weather through the weekend, which would be great, thought Heather, since she hoped to be working with horses on Saturday.

Heather, in her eagerness to talk to Chauncy, was the first one at the bus stop that morning. When the bus arrived and she got on, she was delighted to find that the front seat was not yet taken.

"Hi, Chauncy," she greeted him as she climbed aboard.

"Hi, Heather. Hope you enjoyed the rest of the weekend."

"Yeah, I did."

"Okay, Heather. I suspect you're not sitting up front to talk to me about the weather, right?" Heather nodded. "So," he continued as he drove the bus to its next stop, "did you talk to your parents?"

"Actually, they talked to me. I think they had already decided what the answer was going to be, and fortunately, they said yes! Isn't that great? I'm so excited!" she exclaimed.

"That's wonderful. I think this will be a very good experience for you. But remember, I expect you to work, and the work is hard. Don't assume that all you'll be doing is playing with horses."

"Oh no, Chauncy, I want to work. I hope to have my own horse one day, so I need to learn as much as possible about keeping and taking care of them."

"Good," answered Chauncy. "Then how does this sound? Every Saturday from 9 in the morning until noon? I'll need you to work from 9 until 11, and then for the last hour you can ride. Okay?"

"Sure, that sounds great. I can't wait."

The following Saturday, Heather's mom drove her to Chauncy's, making sure they would arrive a little before 9 a.m. As soon as the car pulled into the driveway, Heather took off her seatbelt, and by the time the car stopped, she was already half way out the door.

"Hey, you! Aren't you forgetting something?" questioned her mom.

"Um...I don't think so."

"Really? You don't know what you're forgetting?"

"No, Mom. What?"

Mrs. Richardson touched her cheek with her hand.

"Oh, I'm sorry," replied Heather. She turned around and kissed her mom on the cheek. "See ya."

"Hold on Heather."

"What Mom?"

"Your father and I will be here at noon to pick you up, okay?

"Okay."

"And don't stay outside if it gets too cold!"

"Sure, Mom. Don't worry. Bye." With that, Heather slammed the door, spun around, and headed toward the house.

"Heather, it's wonderful to see you again. Come in, come in. Would you like some hot chocolate before you get to work?" Mrs. Campbell asked when she answered the door.

"Maybe later, Mrs. Campbell. Right now I'm really anxious to get started."

"Okay, dear. That's fine. Chauncy is at the barn already. Why don't you just go on down."

When Heather reached the barn, she noted that the large sliding door was partially open. As she approached it, she heard a man and woman talking.

"Well I think he's very nice, dear. What do you think?"

"I don't know. It's a big decision. He certainly is beautiful, and we've looked at so many other horses that just don't come close to him. I really don't want to go to more horse farms and keep looking. He's by far the nicest horse we've met."

Heather stopped and tilted her head toward the door so that she could hear the conversation better. Who were they talking about? *Not Immie, please not Immie.*

"Well, folks," came a familiar voice, "I think he's the finest of the group. He's also obviously very fond of you both."

"Okay, then. I think it's settled. Do you agree, Jean?"

"Yes, dear. I can't wait to get him home." There was a pause and then: "Do you want another carrot, Foxy?"

Heather could feel the tension being released from her body. *It isn't Blackjack, I mean Immie, after all. Phew,* she thought. She decided that she had eavesdropped long enough, and forced the sliding door open. As she entered the barn, she saw Chauncy with a tall young man, perhaps in his mid-twenties, and a woman, about the same age, wearing matching red jackets. There was a young bay horse behind them, standing patiently.

"Hi there," said the woman. "Is this your daughter, Chauncy?"

"No, no. This is Heather Richardson. She's my new barn helper."

"Pleased to meet you, Heather," acknowledged the man, reaching his hand toward Heather. "I'm Mr. Kennick, but you can call me Ted. And this is my wife, Jean."

"Hi," came the shy reply.

Chauncy, picking up on Heather's discomfort, broke the silence with a suggestion. "Why don't we go up to the house and fill out the paperwork?"

"What sort of paperwork do we need to do?" asked Mr. Kennick.

"I've got our farm's sales contract that you need to sign. I also need to know how you want his registration form filled out."

"Okay, sounds good," responded Mr. Kennick. Chauncy looked at Heather and told her he'd be back in a couple of minutes. With that, Chauncy, the Kennicks, and the young horse walked out of the barn.

"We'll just lead Foxy back to his pasture first and then..."

The voice faded away. Heather turned and focused her attention on the horses in the barn. Queen was there, head out of the door, looking for Heather's affections.

"Hi there, you pretty little mare," she said softly as she walked over to Queen. She was starting to stroke the mare's neck when she heard a nicker from another stall.

"Blackjack, you're so beautiful," she said as she saw his exotic black head, with a thick, full lock of mane falling between his ears. The stallion's full attention was on her, and she was once again amazed at the beauty of the animal. She approached the horse and said, "How'd you get to be so beautiful, huh? Such a sweetie, too. Do you know that I've been dreaming about you? I know the dreams have been about you because—huh?"

She quickly spun around. She thought she'd heard someone at the door, but fortunately it was just the wind. The last thing she wanted was for anyone, especially Chauncy, to hear her talking about her dream horse. No one else would ever understand. But she knew the horse standing before her would.

She started stroking the gentle stallion's neck, and he responded by lowering his head and resting his neck on the stall door. As she continued to pet him, his eyes grew heavy and he started to drift off to sleep. "I thought you were supposed to be a vicious, man-eating stallion," she said softly. "But you're just a big pussycat."

The rumbling of the sliding door brought both of them back to life.

"Mighty nice folks, the Kennicks. Mighty nice," came a voice from the front of the barn. "Heather, where are you? Oh, there you are. Looks like you've got a favorite already. It doesn't take long," chuckled Chauncy. "Okay, let's get to work before the day is over. I'm in a good mood. Looks like I just sold one of my yearlings. Now then, let's start with the stalls at the end of the barn. Here, bring me the wheelbarrow."

Chauncy quickly explained the finer points of stall cleaning to Heather and put her to work. He turned the radio on and Heather soon lost herself in the music, singing along to every tune. It wasn't long before the first stall was done and she was able to move on to the next one. As she continued, Heather was surprised at the change in the weather; it seemed to be getting somewhat warm. When she mentioned this to Chauncy, he pointed out that she was working up a sweat and that she should take a break.

She decided to take Chauncy's advice and sat down on a bale of hay, leaning against Rusty's stall. She hadn't known that cleaning stalls was so hard. She'd been sitting for about five minutes when suddenly something started nibbling at her head. Looking up, she saw a muzzle and lots of whiskers. She smiled and gently stroked the nose.

"Hi, Rusty. Are you looking for some hay to munch?" she asked. She pulled at the tightly packed bale until she was able to remove a small clump, which she fed to the muzzle above her. The hay disappeared in an instant and the muzzle came back for more. The girl tugged at the bale once again, and this time was able to remove a larger clump.

"You're not going to leave me alone, are you? Oh, all right. One more bit of hay and then I've got to get back to work." She got up off the hay and was then able to remove a full flake. "That's too much," she told Rusty, and tried to put half of it back into the bale. The sound of the rustling hay drew the attention of the other horses, several of whom began to nicker in anticipation of food. "Now we've done it, Rusty. Now everyone wants to be fed."

"Just ignore them," advised Chauncy as he strolled down the aisle, a slight smile on his face. "You'll soon learn that Morgans will do anything for food."

Heather gave a loud groan, forced herself up, and headed back to the wheelbarrow. She set to work and soon lost herself in the music again. Finally, all the stalls were done. Heather, resting against the far wall, glanced over at Immie's stall and panicked when she couldn't see him.

"Chauncy!" she hollered, fearing that something horrible must have happened. She approached the stall just as Chauncy came running down the aisle, and peered inside. There was the stallion, lying on his side, moving his neck through the bedding.

"Something's wrong with him, Chauncy. He was fine and then all of a sudden—"

"Stop worrying," assured Chauncy. "He's fine. He's just rolling."

Hearing voices, the stallion realized he was being watched. With a surge of power, he rolled over and, as his legs came down, they hit the floor with a thud. Then he rose up on his side, waited a moment, and, with a burst of energy, got up. His whole body was covered with shavings, including his mane, forelock, and tail. He looked at the girl, who had been watching in disbelief, and she began to laugh, for instead of looking like a proud and gallant stallion, this horse looked more like a clown, covered as he was from head to tail in shavings. Then the horse put his head down, grunted, and shook himself. When he stopped, Heather could see that most of the shavings had fallen off him, except for those in his mane and tail and a few on his back.

"You've never seen a horse roll before?" asked Chauncy.

"No, never. I thought something was wrong, I'm sorry."

"That's quite all right, Heather. It just goes to show that you are very observant. That's important to me. I know you're on the ball."

Changing the subject, Heather asked, "I'm all done Chauncy, now what do I do?"

"It's time for you to have some fun!" came the reply.

Heather followed her mentor to Rusty's stall. "Put his halter on and bring him up front. I've got a set of cross ties up there."

Heather took the halter off its hook, opened the stall door, and put the halter on Rusty. She then led the horse out of his stall and to the front of the barn, where Chauncy was waiting.

"Right here," said Chauncy, pointing to the cross ties hanging from the wall.

Reaching over to the left, she grabbed the cotton tie and snapped the hook on the end to the side of Rusty's halter. Then she reached over to the tie hanging on the right side and attached that one to the halter.

"Now give him a good brushing."

Heather took a brush from the box that Chauncy had placed on the floor next to her and started brushing the horse. She began on the horse's left shoulder, worked toward his tail, and then continued around the other side until he sparkled. Once Rusty was brushed, Chauncy informed Heather that it was time to tack up.

"I get to ride him?" she exclaimed. She couldn't believe she was actually going to get to ride today.

"Now, what style of riding were you learning last summer?"

"English."

"Hunt or saddle seat?"

"I don't know—what's the difference?"

"Most people learn hunt seat. The saddle has knee rolls and you tend to sit forward a bit. You usually ride in a snaffle bridle with one set of reins, while in saddle seat you ride in a cutback saddle. That's a flatter saddle that makes you sit further back and more upright. You also ride with a full bridle, which has two bits, a snaffle and a curb, and two sets of reins."

"Oh, then I rode hunt seat."

"Okay, I'll get the saddle." Chauncy turned around, disappeared into the tack room, and returned a moment later with a saddle and pad. He handed the off-white fleece pad to Heather, who put it on Rusty's back. Then he handed her the saddle and proceeded to adjust the pad.

"You want the pad up a bit further so that it sits on the withers like this, see? That way the pad will protect the horse's back from the leather of the saddle." He moved the pad to the proper position and then told Heather to put the saddle on. She placed it cautiously on the horse's back, though Rusty seemed oblivious to all the attention. His eyes had closed and his head had started to droop a little. Next, Chauncy took the girth and showed Heather how to properly attach it. Then he once again disappeared into the tack room. When he came back, he had a bridle.

"Okay, now stand on the left side and remove his halter."

Heather started to take off Rusty's halter, but then realized that she would have to remove one of the cross ties first. She reached under the horse's chin and unsnapped the right tie. She was about to take the halter off when something occurred to her.

"Won't he run away if I take the halter off?"

"Well, maybe," replied Chauncy. "Though I think you'd have to wake him up first. But you're right, you never know if a horse might spook or something. It's always best to play it safe. Here, take the reins and slip them over his neck, like this," advised Chauncy. "There, now you can take the halter off and slide the bridle on. That's right, hold the head-stall with your right hand. Now with your left hand guide the bit into his mouth. That's it. Don't worry; he won't bite your finger. Now, try this on," he ordered, handing her a hard hat. "My barn rules require that everyone wear a helmet."

Heather put the helmet on, and secured the chinstrap.

"Now let's go outside," Chauncy said while he walked over to the door and opened it. As the door rumbled open and let in the bright sunlight, Rusty seemed to come to life. Heather led the horse out of the barn and followed Chauncy over to the ring. Once they were inside the ring, Chauncy shut the gate and turned his attention to the girl and horse. He dropped the stirrups, tightened the girth, and then held the horse while Heather mounted. It felt great to be on a horse again, she thought.

"Good boy. Good boy," she said softly, partly to assure the horse and partly to assure herself.

"Okay, the stirrups look like they are a good length for you. Are they comfortable?"

"Yeah, they feel like they are the right length."

"Good. Now, do you remember how to hold the reins?"

"Yup," said Heather as she picked up the reins and adjusted them to the length that she had been taught.

"Here, loosen them up a bit. Rusty goes on a very loose rein; he doesn't like anyone pulling on his mouth. Okay, that looks great. Now, you mentioned that you took lessons for a couple of years. How far along were you?"

"By the end of the second year I was cantering quite a bit and had started jumping. I even went to a small horse show and jumped a whole course of two-foot jumps," Heather announced proudly.

"That's great. Okay, then. Why don't you just take him around by yourself and show me what you know. Make sure you warm him up slowly—walk around several times before you try trotting. Then if all goes well, once he's warmed up you can try cantering. I'll watch you to see how you do, maybe give you a few pointers. Okay? You ready?"

"Yes, I think we're both ready!" Heather answered eagerly.

Chauncy let go of Rusty's bridle and backed away. The bay gelding took a couple of steps toward Chauncy, but Heather gently pulled on the reins and said, "No, no. We don't want to run Chauncy over. Let's go this way." She pulled back slightly on the right rein so that the horse's head turned to the right, then she squeezed with her legs. Rusty responded by moving forward. They walked off toward the rail and quickly straightened out. The ring wasn't very large, certainly nothing like the huge indoor arena in which Heather learned to ride. But it looked big enough in which to do a comfortable canter, and that was all that she cared about.

Rusty moved out at a fast pace. He didn't try to break into a trot, but his walk was brisk and energetic. The movement of the animal under her felt wonderful, as did the crisp air, and the creak of the leather. Before she knew it, the two of them had already been around the ring twice.

"Now let me see you do a circle," commanded her new instructor.

Heather pulled back slightly on the left rein while releasing just a bit with the right. The horse turned his head to the left and his body followed as the two of them performed a perfect little circle. Then Heather confidently guided him back to the rail. They continued on until that same voice instructed them to stop. She pulled back on both reins and Rusty didn't just stop, but started to back up.

"Not so hard, Heather. Okay, release the reins. That's right. He's got a very soft mouth. That means he's very receptive to the slightest pressure on the bit, so you don't have to pull as hard as you did with the lesson horses. Try it again. Move forward and when you're ready, try stopping again."

Heather obliged. She moved forward about ten feet and then asked the horse to stop again. But this time she didn't pull as hard. Rusty came to a quick stop without backing up.

"Great! That's it! Now let's see you reverse and walk the other way."

Heather turned the horse and continued in the other direction. *This is fun!* she thought. Rusty was much more responsive than the lesson horses, and she was going to have to get used to being lighter with her hands. She smiled and reached forward just a bit so she could pet him with her right hand.

"Good boy, you're such a good boy," she praised him as she patted his neck. Rusty's right ear rotated slightly so that he could hear what Heather was saying. They continued walking until they were interrupted once again by Chauncy.

"Okay, are you ready to trot?"

"Yup, I think we are."

"Good, just cluck to him and squeeze a little with your legs. You don't have to kick him. If you do kick him, he's more likely to break into a canter. Ready? Give it a try when you feel ready."

Heather let Rusty walk halfway around the ring before asking him to trot.

"Okay, boy, let's give it a try," she whispered to him. She clucked and squeezed her legs ... but nothing happened.

"Try again," encouraged Chauncy. "Squeeze a little harder."

Heather gave it another try, but again, nothing happened.

"Again," said Chauncy.

Heather squeezed harder and clucked louder, and this time Rusty broke into a trot right away.

"He just has to get used to you," said Chauncy. "Before you know it, you'll be reading each other's minds."

After the girl had taken the horse around the ring several times, Chauncy asked them to stop, reverse, and trot in the other direction. The horse was obviously getting used to his rider, since he now responded quickly to her requests.

"Okay, Heather, why don't you walk him now? Give him a little breather. We certainly don't want him to break into a sweat in this cold weather."

"Whoa, easy, Rusty" came the command. Rusty immediately slowed to a walk. "He's not even breathing hard, Chauncy," noted Heather.

"No, he's in pretty good shape considering the fact that I haven't done much with him lately."

After he watched her walking Rusty for several minutes, Chauncy asked Heather, "Are you ready to try cantering? You don't have to if you don't want to. It doesn't matter to me, so don't push yourself if you feel you're not ready."

"I'd like to try it. I think we can do it!" responded a very enthusiastic Heather as she continued to walk the horse.

"Do you remember how to ask for a canter?" her instructor inquired.

"Pull back on the outside rein and kick the horse with the outside leg at the same time?"

"Right, but you should only pull back on the rein very slightly—so slight that I shouldn't be able to notice it—while at the same time just tapping him lightly with your outside leg. Remember, he's used to very subtle commands, and if you're too heavy-handed he'll get upset. You think you can do it?"

"I'm pretty sure I can," answered Heather.

"Okay, give it a try."

Heather pulled back on the right rein and squeezed with her right leg ... but Rusty continued to walk. Nothing happened.

"No, no, that's not right," Chauncy gently admonished her. "See how you've pulled his head to the right? That's too much. Loosen the right rein a bit. Right. Now, tap him with your right leg and tell him, in a commanding voice, 'canter.' Go ahead, give it a try."

"Canter," Heather ordered as she tapped Rusty with the heel of her boot.

The front end of the horse's body immediately rose up a bit as he broke into a canter. Heather was startled at the response, and lost her balance slightly. She grabbed Rusty's mane with both hands as he came down, his left leg leading the way. Up and down, up and down, in a rocking horse motion he went, and Heather was unable to regain her balance. After three strides, the horse stopped.

"What's he doing?" Heather asked.

"He knows you're having trouble, so he stopped. Rusty is a great babysitter and will take care of you. He's just waiting for you to regain your balance. Are you okay?"

"Yeah, I'm just not used to that I guess. The horses I used to ride moved forward, not up, when asked to canter. Can I try again?"

"Go ahead, if you feel comfortable."

Heather once again asked Rusty to canter, but this time she was ready for the up and down motion of the Morgan, and managed to maintain her balance—although it was hard at first. After a couple of times around the ring, though, she was able to relax and her body began to rock along with the horse. A few more times around the ring and she asked Rusty to stop. When he did, she reversed him and asked him to canter again. He immediately picked up the cue, and they were off.

"Now you've got it!" exclaimed Chauncy. "You guys look great together!"

A huge smile grew on Heather's face as she realized that she and this beautiful Morgan were riding together, communicating with one another. What a great feeling! Rusty's canter, once she was used to it, was wonderful. The up and down motion gave the canter an airy feeling, almost as if they were flying. After a few times around the ring, she brought Rusty back to a walk. Then, with the smile still plastered on her face, she trotted over to Chauncy, who took his glove off and felt the horse's chest.

"He's not very warm, but why don't you walk him around for about ten minutes. I'll meet you in the barn. When you're done, just dismount in the ring and then bring him back into the barn."

"Okay, Chauncy," Heather said as she turned Rusty away from him and began to walk around the ring.

"By the way, Heather," Chauncy said before walking away, "that was a really good job, and I'm not just saying that. I can tell by watching you that you are a natural rider. I think you'll get along great with my horses."

Heather was a bit stunned by such praise, and put it aside as Chauncy just being nice to her. She loosened her reins and continued walking Rusty, all the while talking to him, telling him what a wonderful horse he was and how much fun they were going to have together. Once he seemed completely cooled down, she dismounted and took him back to the barn. The door was open and Chauncy was busy sweeping the aisle.

"Just put him on the cross ties, take off his tack, and give him a good brushing. Then you can put him away. I've already put a flake of hay in his stall."

Heather did as she was told and quickly had the horse put back in his stall. Then she took off her hard hat, returned it to the tack room, and asked Chauncy if he needed anything else done.

"Nope," came the response. "I think that's enough for one day. Besides, your mother will be here any minute."

"It's 12 o'clock already?" asked a very surprised Heather.

"Yup, time to go," Chauncy answered as he turned and headed out of the barn. Heather followed, and as they approached the house, her parents drove up.

"Thanks so much. I had a blast," Heather said as she veered off the path to walk toward her parents' car. "I can't wait till next week."

"Well I'm glad you enjoyed yourself, Heather. Have a good weekend. I'll see you on Monday."

"Okay, thanks again," Heather replied as she jumped into the waiting car, anxious to tell her parents all about her morning.

THE TROUBLESOME CANTER

A s February melted into March, Heather kept herself quite busy. She continued to spend every Saturday morning at Chauncy's farm, looking forward to each visit with great anticipation. She had managed to keep her grades up and, in fact, had improved them slightly. Her parents attributed this to her desire to continue working at the farm. Regardless of the reason, they were very happy to see their daughter doing well, and therefore encouraged her involvement with the horses.

Heather was so fixated on her new horse endeavor that when her birthday rolled around, there was only one thing she wanted.

"Don't you want a new outfit or maybe a gift certificate to one of your favorite stores?" asked Mrs. Richardson.

"Nope, just a halter for Blackjack."

So for her sweet sixteenth birthday, Heather was presented with a new leather halter. And as a joke, Chauncy gave her a new, stainless steel pitchfork.

By early March, Heather had started teaching Rusty to jump. Chauncy didn't have the heart to tell Heather that the horse was already a jumping champion, because the girl was so pleased with her achievement. But Heather's first love was still the black stallion. After her chores were done, she would bring him up to the cross ties and spend close to half an hour just brushing him. The stallion obviously loved the attention. Never one to fall asleep while being groomed, the horse would watch the girl's every move and, when taken off the ties, would nuzzle her, as if to say "thank you." She was now calling the horse by his new barn name, Blackjack. Chauncy had heard her call the stallion Blackjack so many times that he finally asked her about it. Rather embarrassed, she told him about the dream, but to her relief Chauncy didn't laugh or make fun of her. He very nicely explained, "Sometimes dreams have a way of telling us something important." He didn't seem to mind at all, and the horse took to the name immediately.

One morning, while Heather was playing with the stallion, Chauncy came into the barn. He had something important to ask Heather.

"I was wondering," he said, "if you would like to ride Blackjack?"

Heather, shocked and excited by this question, stopped what she was doing but didn't answer.

"I've been watching how well you've been doing with Rusty," continued her mentor, "and I think you can handle Blackjack. I want to see what the two of you can do together. I've been working him in harness to get ready for the Futurity in June, but it occurred to me that in order for Blackjack to have a chance at the grand championship, he'll have to go in a saddle class. He doesn't have to win the class, but he has to do well enough to place. I can't ride him because I'm not exactly, well, shall we say, graceful in the saddle? He's been started under saddle, and goes really well except for a problem with picking up the right lead. If you can get him going and work through his problem, then I think we've got a shot at the championship. What do you say? Do you want to give it a try?"

Heather was quiet for a moment. Unlike the other opportunities that Chauncy had offered in the past, this offer carried a lot of responsibility. She didn't want to disappoint Chauncy or get his hopes up only to have them dashed by her mistakes. She looked at Blackjack, who was watching the two of them intently, and rubbed his forehead.

"What do you think, Blackjack? Can we do it?"

"Of course," Chauncy cautioned, "you'll have to ride him saddle seat, which means a cutback saddle and a full bridle. It's completely different from what you're used to. If you want, you can use Rusty to practice on with the different saddle and bridle. In fact, I think it would be a good idea. He's much more forgiving than Blackjack, and you're used to him. So do you want to give it a try?"

"Okay, Chauncy," Heather replied somewhat hesitantly. "But I don't want to let you down. What if I can't get him to canter correctly?"

"Then I'll just have to rethink this whole thing. I certainly won't be upset with you, because you've done a great job here and I realize I'm asking a lot."

"I'll give it a try," Heather said, smiling weakly.

"Great! Then let's get started. Are you ready for your first saddle seat lesson with Rusty?"

With Chauncy's help, Heather got Rusty ready. Leading the gelding out to the ring, the girl noticed the horse was wearing what Chauncy had referred to as a 'full bridle,' which meant that it had two bits and two sets of reins.

"What the heck do I do with these?" she asked herself as she collected both sets of reins and put them over the horse's head. Then she dropped the stirrups on the strange saddle and mounted. The saddle was much flatter than her hunt saddle, with no knee rolls but large, flat flaps instead. There was a small opening at the front of the saddle, which according to Chauncy, was how the saddle got its name. The original saddles were 'cut back' so as not to interfere with high-withered horses.

"This feels really weird!" exclaimed the young rider.

"It will definitely take some getting used to," Chauncy agreed.

The elderly instructor then showed the girl how to properly hold the reins and sit in this new saddle. He had her walk Rusty around the ring, so she could slowly get used to the saddle and bridle. They walked for a bit, and then trotted and even

70

tried a brief canter. At the end of their lesson, Heather gratefully slid off the horse. Her upper leg muscles were aching from all the use. With a smile, she turned to Chauncy and announced, "I think I'm going to be walking funny tomorrow!"

Heather now had a new mission. She practiced riding saddle seat every Saturday with Rusty, in anticipation of working with Blackjack. Then, on a particularly nice spring day, she was grooming the stallion when Chauncy came into the barn. It was a beautiful morning, the flowers were beginning to bloom and the birds were chirping. The barn was empty except for Rusty, Blackjack, and Heather.

"Have you finished your chores already?" Chauncy asked.

"Yup," Heather replied, not looking away from her charge.

"Well, I've got a surprise for you today," he announced.

That caught the girl's attention, and she eagerly asked him what the surprise was.

"Are you finished grooming him yet?"

"I am now!" Heather replied, thinking that she'd get the surprise as soon as she finished playing with Blackjack.

"Okay, tack him up!" Chauncy commanded.

"You're kidding, right? You don't really mean that I can ride him, do you?"

"Yes, I really do mean that you can ride him. You've made great progress with Rusty, and I think you are now ready to ride Blackjack."

Heather was unable to contain her excitement. With Chauncy's help, she quickly got the horse saddled and bridled. Chauncy led the horse out to the ring while Heather grabbed her helmet and followed along. Her heart began to pound wildly as they approached the ring and she realized that she was about to ride her dream horse.

They walked through the gate and Heather shut it as Chauncy led Blackjack to the middle of the enclosure. He adjusted the saddle and then motioned for Heather to hop aboard. She put on her helmet, mustered up all her courage, and mounted the stallion. Blackjack took a step forward, anxious to go.

"Whoa, boy, not yet," she commanded, gathering up the reins and looking at Chauncy.

"You ready, Heather?"

"Yup," replied the girl, trying to sound confident.

"Okay, just walk around the ring. It's going to take him a little while to get used to you."

Heather clucked to Blackjack and moved her hands forward slightly, hoping that was enough to get him going. The stallion cocked his right ear back toward her ... but didn't move.

"That's okay, try again."

Heather repeated her actions, this time adding a few words of encouragement.

"Come on, boy. Don't make me look foolish now." Blackjack took two steps forward and then broke into a trot.

"Whoa," pleaded Heather, surprised at the horse's reaction. She pulled on the reins, much more than the horse was used to, and he reacted to this first by stopping, and then by raising his head up as high as he could.

Suddenly he started to go forward again.

"No, boy, that's not what I want. You're supposed to be—"

"Heather," Chauncy interrupted, "take your lower leg off him. Then he should relax."

Heather did as she was told, and the horse immediately relaxed.

"Remember, he's been trained as a saddle seat horse. That means he's not used to having lots of lower leg pressure on him. Okay, now try again. Ask him to walk, but be careful. No leg."

The girl asked the horse to walk again, and this time was rewarded with a true walk. She whispered to her steed, "We can do it. I know we can," as she reached down to his neck and patted him with her right hand.

"Heather, relax, you're fine. Take a couple of deep breaths. Good, now he can feel you relaxing

73

and he'll relax too. Great. Now just walk him around for a while. Try turning him, stopping him, and just getting used to his feel."

Heather obediently followed Chauncy's commands. She walked Blackjack slowly around the ring, all the while looking down at the horse's neck, completely oblivious to the rest of the world. Then she asked him to stop without using her voice. She wanted to see if the horse would respond to very light cues. The horse quietly stopped.

"Great, now make him stand there for a minute."

Heather complied, but Blackjack did not appreciate the request. He began to paw with his right leg, much to Heather's embarrassment.

"That's okay, he's just feeling you out. He wants to know what he can get away with. Stallions will do that a lot."

Heather managed to force a smile as the horse continued to paw.

"Okay, that's enough. Don't let him continue pawing. Tell him 'no,' and snap the reins just once."

"No!" the girl ordered as sternly as possible, tugging once at the reins.

The horse stopped his pawing.

"Okay, now continue walking for a bit and then try stopping again. If he starts to paw again, don't wait; tell him 'no' right away. He's got to know that you're the boss. And don't forget to breathe!"

Heather let out a slight laugh.

"Okay, now stop."

Heather pulled slightly on the reins. Blackjack stopped right away. Relieved that the horse wasn't pawing, Heather looked at Chauncy and started to smile. As she did so, the horse began to paw. She rolled her eyes as if to say, "Geeze, will you stop already?" and turned her attention immediately to her mount. She snapped the reins and ordered, "No!"

The horse stopped pawing and turned an ear back toward his rider.

"Perfect, now you've got his attention. Now see if you can get him to back up."

Heather gathered up the reins and pulled lightly, then released, pulled and released. Blackjack flexed his head and slowly began to back up. He continued to back until Heather released the reins, at which point he stopped. She waited a few moments and then asked him to go forward. She had started to relax, and the horse, sensing his rider's new-found confidence, relaxed too. They walked forward and then made several small circles, some to the right and some to the left. They cut through the center of the ring and even walked diagonally across it, coming so close to Chauncy that he had to move out of their way. "Oops" was the only sound Heather made as she brushed passed her instructor, a permanent smile now plastered on her face.

"I think you're ready to try trotting now. Do you feel ready?"

"Yeah, I'll give it a try."

"Just squeeze your upper legs slightly and cluck to him. Ready?"

"Yup."

"Okay, whenever you feel right, tell him to trot."

Heather gathered up all her courage and asked for a trot. Blackjack responded by immediately breaking into a trot. The quick response caught Heather off guard, and in order to maintain her balance, she grabbed him with her lower legs. The horse instantly sped up, which caused Heather to cling even tighter with her legs. Blackjack threw his head up in defiance and broke into a canter.

"Whoa, whoa. Easy Blackjack," Heather ordered as calmly as possible. The horse settled down and continued to canter for several strides until Heather was able to regain her balance. Then she pulled back gently on the reins, and the horse broke down to a trot. *Get your legs off him,* she kept telling herself.

With all her concentration on her legs, Heather forgot to look where she was going, and the horse started to cut into the center of the ring.

"Keep him on the rail, Heather. You're doing great. Just relax. You've got him now, right there, that's perfect!"

"He feels fantastic!" Heather shouted gleefully, amazed at the smoothness of the horse's trot.

"Don't let him slow down. Cluck to him. Yup, that's it."

Heather and Blackjack continued going around the ring. The horse's long mane blew back past his rider's hands while his thick, upright neck brought his head level with Heather's.

"Try bringing him across the center of the ring so that you can reverse directions," Chauncy suggested.

Heather obeyed, and as she trotted down the rail, turned the horse and cut easily across the center to reverse directions. She continued to trot around the ring several times and would have continued forever, but fortunately, Chauncy was keeping a close eye on the pair and reminded her that Blackjack was getting tired. She brought him back to a walk and then rode the horse to the center, where her instructor was waiting.

"You did really well, Heather. How do you feel about it?"

"I was pretty nervous at first but I think we did okay. He's a neat horse."

"He's really special, and you look very good on him. I think you make a nice pair. With a little work, I think you two could really 'wow' the judges. Are you game?"

"Yeah, I'd really like to give it a try. Can we try cantering now? The little bit of cantering that he did felt really smooth, like a rocking horse. I'd like to try doing it all the way around the ring."

"Actually, I'd prefer that you wait to canter. I'd like you to be a little more comfortable on Blackjack first. Why don't you cool him out now."

"Okay," answered a slightly disappointed Heather.

Over the next few weeks, Heather continued working Blackjack as much as possible. Seeing how excited she was about the possibility of showing the horse, her mom had even agreed to drive her to the barn every day after school. By the middle of April, Chauncy had decided she was ready to try cantering.

Blackjack stood patiently on the cross ties as Heather groomed him, all the while talking to him about what a good horse he was. Chauncy was very pleased with the bond the two had formed. The nervousness that Heather had shown the first time she rode Blackjack was gone, replaced by confidence. The confidence was transmitted to the horse, who apparently adored Heather, since he'd follow her around the ring like a puppy when she dismounted, reins dangling loosely from his neck.

Chauncy could only hope that this trust would help overcome the difficulties that the stallion had with cantering on his right lead. He had taught the horse to drive himself and then sent him to a professional trainer to be broken to saddle. The trainer had remarked on the amazing willingness of the horse to learn, and how pleased he was with Blackjack.

Then, a week before the horse was to return home, a passing car blew a tire as it drove past the arena where he was being ridden. The horse had just been asked to canter on the right lead when the loud blast of the tire and the resultant screeching of the brakes caught the animal by surprise. Blackjack was terrified, and began to buck violently. The trainer, also caught off guard, was thrown from the horse.

Fortunately, neither horse nor rider was injured, and the trainer was able to get up as his assistant came running into the arena. They caught the frightened horse, who stood quietly shaking while they tried to calm him down. After checking him over, they put him back in his stall and resumed his training the next day. But the horse started bucking whenever asked to canter on the right lead. The trainer kept Blackjack for an extra month in an attempt to get him over his fear, but to no avail. In fact, the problem seemed to be getting worse. It was decided that the best thing to do was return the horse to Chauncy and hope that time would heal the stallion's emotional scar.

"Okay, Heather, here's the plan," Chauncy informed her as he walked beside her and Blackjack toward the ring. "Warm him up first for about 15 minutes. Walk him and then do some trotting both ways. When you feel ready, ask him to canter on the left lead. But when it's time to try the right lead, instead of asking for it from a walk, go into a trot and then just urge him on to a canter. I think that's the best way to do it this first time."

"Okay, Chauncy. Don't worry, we'll be fine," Heather answered. She mounted the horse and began warming him up. After walking and trotting both ways for about 20 minutes, she told her instructor that she was ready to try cantering.

"Whenever you're ready, then, give it a try."

Blackjack was walking quietly, somewhat distracted by a small swallow that had landed on the gate. Heather pulled her right hand back ever so slightly, tapped Blackjack with her right heel and gave the command "Canter." Instantly the horse broke into a canter. It was a bit fast, but Heather didn't mind; she was thrilled that the horse had obeyed her.

"Great, now slow him down just a bit and then continue around the ring several times. Try and get a feel for his canter."

Heather grew more confident as they cantered around the ring. The gait was so smooth that it was as if she were on a floating horse. After they had gone around the ring several times, Chauncy told her to bring the horse back down to a walk and reverse. The horse obediently came back to a walk, but when they reversed, he pinned his ears back and started swishing his tail—a sign of annoyance.

"What's wrong with him?" Heather asked, concerned that she had done something wrong.

"Nothing except that he's anticipating. He knows that once you've cantered to the left, you'll want to canter to the right. He's letting you know he's not happy. Just talk to him. When you're ready, ask for a trot."

"Good boy, easy, easy. There's nothing wrong. Come on, relax," Heather whispered. Blackjack responded by putting his head down a bit and relaxing his tail. His ears were slower to respond, but by the time they had walked around the ring once, they were again forward. Heather had him walk around the ring once more, and then asked for a trot. The horse seemed surprised and, in fact, hesitated a bit before obeying. Once they were trotting, Chauncy told her to urge him on by using her legs and voice. Blackjack increased his speed until he was going so fast that Heather had trouble maintaining her position.

"Keep asking him for more speed, Heather. He doesn't want to canter and will do all he can to avoid it. That's it, he's thinking about it."

"Come on boy, let's go, come on!" Heather urged as she squeezed her legs with all her strength. Unable to trot any faster, Blackjack pinned his ears back and broke into a canter. His first few strides were partially bucks, but he didn't stop.

"Beautiful! You did it!" came a gleeful voice. "That's great! Now don't let him stop, urge him on. It's okay if it's fast right now!"

"Come on, Blackjack, keep going," Heather ordered. After three strides, Blackjack had stopped bucking and cantered along just as nicely as he had to the left, although his ears were still pinned back.

"Give him lots of praise," ordered Chauncy. "And then stop and get off him."

Heather readily complied. "We did it, Chauncy!" she exclaimed as she hopped off.

"That was fantastic! I knew you could do it."

"But why'd I have to get off so quickly?"

"Once a horse does something right like he just did, you want to get off him right away as a reward. He'll remember that and want to get the same reward next time. So just walk him around until he's cooled off, and then come to the house. We need to talk."

Heather just looked at Chauncy as he walked away. *Oh, no, now what?* she wondered.

After Blackjack was put back in his stall, Heather strolled up to the house and knocked on the door.

"Oh, Heather dear, how nice to see you," Mrs. Campbell greeted her as she opened the door.

"Mr. Campbell wanted to see me about something."

"Oh yes, he told me. Would you like a brownie? I just made them."

"Yes, thank you."

Heather followed Mrs. Campbell into the kitchen. She took a brownie and a glass of milk and sat down at the table.

"Oh there you are, Heather," Chauncy said as he came into the room. "I asked you in so that you could try on my daughter's saddle suits. There are three to choose from and one of them should fit you. I've laid them out in the guest room if you'd like to go try them on."

Relieved that all Chauncy wanted was for her to try on a show outfit, Heather finished her brownie and then tried on the suits. One suit was dark brown and the other two were navy blue. The brown suit and one of the navy suits were much too large, but the third suit fit her pretty well. The pants were a bit loose, but Mrs. Campbell suggested that a belt would take care of that, while the jacket sleeves would have to be shortened about an inch. Mrs. Campbell volunteered to do the work after her husband glowingly praised the amazing sewing capabilities of his wife. Then Chauncy pulled a hat out of a box and put it on Heather's head.

"I have to wear that, too?"

"It's called a derby, and yes, you do have to wear it. Fortunately it fits you fine. You'll have to have your hair pulled back and also wear these boots," Chauncy said as he pulled a pair of short black boots out of another box.

Just then, the doorbell rang and everyone turned toward the door.

"Hello, anyone home?" came a voice.

"Hi, Mom, we're in here. You gotta see this!" Heather shouted.

A moment later, Mrs. Richardson came in. "Oh my, Heather, you look, well, umm, very, very English."

"Thanks a lot, Mom. This is a saddle suit. It's for the show."

"That's what I figured. I've just never seen you so dressed up before. How'd it go today? Were you able to get the horse to run?"

Chauncy and Heather smiled at each other. "No, Mom, not run, canter. And yes, we did. It went really well."

"Wonderful, dear. Now I hate to rush you, but your dad is in the car and you know that he doesn't like to be kept waiting!"

"Okay, I'll be ready in a couple of minutes," Heather said as she turned and headed toward the guest room to change.

Heather continued to work Blackjack for several weeks and was able to get him to canter from a trot without much trouble. Finally, she and Chauncy agreed it was time to try to get him to canter on the right lead from a walk. After all, the big show was only a month away and he would have to pick up the canter from a walk in the show ring. Heather put the horse through his paces, asking for trots both ways and then for the canter on the left lead. When it came time to ask for a right lead canter, Blackjack apparently thought that he would be asked to canter from a trot again, since he started to trot without being asked.

"No, boy, that's not what I want," Heather said as she brought him back to a walk.

The horse seemed a bit agitated, but he was still listening to his rider. Heather then asked for a canter from the walk. Blackjack pinned his ears back, but this time he also started backing up and swishing his tail in annoyance. She asked for a canter again, and the horse backed up even faster.

"Don't give up, Heather. Ask him again. He knows you're not going to hurt him," Chauncy instructed as he approached the pair, urging the horse on. "Come on, Blackjack, canter!"

The horse continued to back up, until Chauncy grabbed the reins and pulled forward on them. This stopped the horse from backing, and seemed to relax him a bit, too. Chauncy let go of the reins and Heather again asked for a canter.

Immediately, the horse broke into a canter.

"Praise him, praise him!" Chauncy shouted over the thunder of the horse's hooves.

"Good boy, you did it, you did it!" Heather told her mount as they cantered around the ring. She was thrilled that they had finally managed to canter from a walk, but with the show just weeks away, how would they ever repeat that feat in the show ring?

THE MORGAN
HORSE SHOW

Heather was now riding every day after school, and everything was coming together except for the cantering.

Chauncy thought that the young girl and her horse looked beautiful, confident, and elegant. And the ride would always go well ... until it was time to canter on the right lead. Sometimes Blackjack would pick up the canter without backing, but usually Chauncy had to grab the reins and move the pair forward before the horse would cooperate. And without fail, Blackjack would pin his ears and swish his tail in annoyance—something Chauncy had told Heather the judges did not like. But still, Chauncy was very pleased with their progress. It was a huge improvement over the bucking and outright refusals the horse had given the trainer, and Chauncy felt that with any luck, they would be okay in the show ring.

The show was a weeklong extravaganza. It began on Monday with a "Welcome to the Show" party and ended on Saturday with a "Hope to See You Next Year" party. In between, there were all sorts of classes that made use of the Morgan's versatility. These classes included in-hand, pleasure saddle, pleasure driving, park horse, jumping, trotting races, dressage, hunter pleasure, trail, carriage, and even a costume class for the youngsters, as well as the Futurity classes. Blackjack's first class would be the Futurity in-hand class on Wednesday morning, followed by his pleasure driving class on Friday and then the saddle class on Saturday afternoon. Saturday night, which was when all the final championship classes were held, was also the night that the Futurity grand champion would be pinned—amid much fanfare.

When the week of the show finally arrived, Chauncy took Blackjack to the fairgrounds on Monday to give him a chance to settle in before his first class. He had decided to stable the horse with a good friend of his, Tom MacDonald. Tom was a well-known and well-respected trainer who would be busy all week showing his clients' horses, as well as showing Blackjack in the in-hand class. The outside of Mr. MacDonald's stalls were decorated with dark blue curtains with gray trim, and on each curtain the words "Tom MacDonald Training Stable" were embroidered in the same shade of gray as the trim.

The morning of the in-hand class, Heather arrived and approached the first young woman she saw, looking for Blackjack's stall. "Excuse me," she said.

The young woman, in her early twenties, was dressed in very grungy looking jeans and had hair that probably had not seen a brush in a long time. But she looked like she knew her way around.

"I'm looking for Mr. Campbell, who is supposed to be stabled with you guys. He has a horse that is showing—"

"Oh yeah" came the response in a very gruff but friendly voice. "You mean Chauncy. He's in the prep stall with his horse right now. It's that middle stall right there," the groom said, pointing to a stall off to the left.

"Thanks," Heather responded. She and her mom walked toward the prep stall.

"Chauncy?" Heather asked as she peered into the stall.

"Heather! I'm glad you could make it. Come on in and tell me what you think of our boy. Looks pretty good, huh?" exclaimed a very excited Chauncy.

Heather cautiously stepped into the stall. What she saw amazed her. Blackjack was standing patiently on the cross ties while two people were busy putting the finishing touches on him. Heather knew that Blackjack was a beautiful horse, but she had never seen him sparkle so. His hooves were painted jet black and had such a shiny gloss that Heather could actually see her reflection in them, while his coat positively glistened.

"There, how's that?" asked the groom who had been working on Blackjack's hooves as she stood up. She held a small jar that contained hoof polish, some of which dripped down the sides of the jar. The hands of the groom also sported numerous black patches, obviously from an overzealous application of the polish.

"Looks great," answered the man who was standing in the back corner of the stall next to Chauncy. "Why don't you just put a little baby oil around his eyes and nostrils? We've got to go in another five minutes."

"Did they announce our class already?" the other groom asked, a bit worried. "I didn't hear anything."

"Yeah," answered the first groom. "They just gave the ten-minute call."

"Heather," Chauncy said, pulling the girl's attention away from the grooms, "this is Tom MacDonald. He will be showing Blackjack for us today."

"Nice to meet you, Mr. MacDonald," Heather said, holding out her hand.

"Nice to meet you too, Heather," Mr. MacDonald replied as he shook Heather's hand. "I've heard a lot of nice things about you."

Mr. MacDonald was a handsome man—tall, thin, and probably about 45 years old, she guessed. His hair was beginning to gray around the edges and his face was starting to show the wear that years of hard work out in the sun had caused. Still, she thought, there was a very gentle look to him.

"Uh oh." Heather smiled, a bit uncomfortable at the thought of somebody talking about her horse skills.

"Don't worry, it was all good," Mr. MacDonald assured her. "Chauncy told me how you were able to get this guy to finally canter. I also happen to know that Chauncy thinks very highly of you, because he wouldn't change this horse's barn name for just anybody!"

"Five-minute call for class 52, Futurity Three-Year-Old In-Hand," interrupted a loud voice, coming from the speakers outside.

"Tammy, grab the bridle," Mr. MacDonald instructed.

"Here it is," came the reply as one of the grooms handed the trainer a handsome leather bridle. Unlike the bridle that Heather used for riding, the in-hand bridle only had one bit and one set of reins. The noseband and browband were red patent leather, with a thin black line in the center. The tack looked really striking on Blackjack's beautiful head. As soon as the bridle was on, Mr. MacDonald asked everyone to leave the stall. Once they'd vacated the area, he and Blackjack came out. Instantly, Heather's beloved horse came to life. He walked forward majestically, head held high upon a gorgeous, upright neck. He gave out a loud whinny and everyone laughed.

"Where's Jill?" Mr. MacDonald asked no one in particular.

"Here I am," came the reply as yet another young woman in her early twenties came running up. She was dressed in off-white chinos and a red polo shirt, which matched Mr. MacDonald's outfit.

"You're tailing, right?" the trainer asked.

"Yeah."

"Chauncy, what's that mean?" Heather asked.

"She's going in the ring with Mr. MacDonald to help him show the horse. When they lead the horse down the rail at a trot, she'll be behind and off to the side, hence the name 'tailer.' It helps to keep the horse on the rail."

Everyone quietly followed the trainer and his charge to the grandstand ring. When they arrived, Heather saw a number of horses standing around, quietly waiting for their turn to enter the ring. Mr. MacDonald picked a place to wait for the class away from the other horses. As soon as he stopped, the grooms set to work cleaning the horse one last time. Heather couldn't believe the attention paid to grooming, and watched as every part of the horse's body was checked for specks of dirt. The previous class had already been pinned, and the competitors were now leaving the ring through the out-gate at the other end of the ring. A burly looking man standing by the in-gate then opened it, and the announcer's voice blasted through the loud speakers.

"Class 52, Futurity Three-Year-Old In-Hand, please enter the ring."

Suddenly, 15 horses came to life. Trainers' voices rose above the whinnies and snorts with commands of "Come on," "Hut, hut," "Up now," "Let's go," "Get up" and all sorts of other instructions, given to get the horses' attention. Just like the others, Blackjack seemed to grow several inches as he puffed himself up and trotted next to Mr. MacDonald into the ring.

Heather had never seen a ring full of more beautiful horses. Most of them were bay, but there were also three chestnuts. Blackjack was the only black horse, and he really stood out. Mr. MacDonald and Blackjack were the fifth team in line as they followed the leaders around the ring. There was a photographer in the center as well as a ringmaster—a man in a bright red riding coat telling the exhibitors where to line up their horses.

Once all of the horses were positioned, the judge motioned to the first trainer to bring his horse to the center of the ring. Once there, the trainer posed the horse in what Chauncy explained to Mrs. Richardson as a "stretched position," his hind legs slightly back and front legs perpendicular to the ground. Heather nodded in agreement as Chauncy spoke; it was the same show pose that Blackjack had taken on that cold winter day when they first met. Turning her attention back to the ring, she saw that the horse was a beautiful bay stallion, with the most amazing tail. It was so long that it actually touched the ground. The judge walked over to the horse and then quickly made his way around the animal, scrutinizing every single part of him. He stepped back and nodded at the trainer. Apparently the trainer knew what the judge wanted, since he immediately led the horse to the far wall and trotted him down the rail. As the horse began to trot, several people in the audience started hooting and hollering as loudly as they could.

The judge carefully watched the horse trot down the rail, glanced at his clipboard, and wrote something on it. Then he turned his attention to the next horse. The class went at a brisk pace, and before Heather knew it, it was Blackjack's turn. Heather was so proud of her horse. He held his head high upon his upright neck, and it appeared as though he had puffed his chest out about three times its normal size. He pranced toward the judge, and at Mr. MacDonald's cue, put himself into the show stretch about which Chauncy had spoken. Immediately, Chauncy, the grooms, and Heather began to cheer.

Once the judge was finished looking over Blackjack, he motioned to Mr. MacDonald, who led the horse to the rail and trotted to the far end, much to the satisfaction of the audience. Quite a few onlookers had started to cheer for Blackjack, whom they apparently felt was a top contender in the class.

When all of the horses had had a chance to preen, the judge stepped back so that he could see them as a group. Then he motioned to the first horse in line. Immediately several fans of this horse began to applaud as the trainer led the horse to the center of the ring.

"What's the judge doing, Chauncy?" Heather asked.

"He's picking out his final eight horses, the ones that will get ribbons. He'll pick eight horses to come to the center and then pin his class from that group."

As they talked, more cheers arose from the spectators. Heather turned to look at the horses and saw Blackjack strutting out toward the center of the ring.

"He's going to get a ribbon!" Heather exclaimed.

The judge pulled six other horses out of the original lineup. As soon as the eight finalists were lined up, the audience became rather boisterous. People were yelling and screaming and banging on the rail. The louder the noise got, the more the horses seemed to enjoy themselves. They knew they were showing off to the crowd and that they were indeed special. The judge again looked over the horses, quickly glancing at each one. He went down the lineup and then walked back up. He stopped at Blackjack, looked him over, and then went around him to look at the other side. Then he looked at the horse in front of Blackjack, the one who was first in line. This horse too, was looked at from both sides.

Finally, the judge motioned to Mr. MacDonald to bring Blackjack to the front of the line. The crowd went wild. The judge took one last look at the whole group, scribbled something on his clipboard and then handed it to the ringmaster. The crowd stopped cheering and the horses seemed to sense that the judging was over. They lowered their heads and stopped stretching, while the trainers started talking to one another. After a couple of minutes, the announcer's voice blasted through the speakers.

"Ladies and gentlemen, we have the results for class number 52. First place goes to—" There was a slight pause, as if to build suspense. "—Number 142, Gallant Image, owned by Mr. Chauncy Campbell and shown by Mr. Tom MacDonald."

As soon as the winner was called out, the spectators once again began to cheer. Mr. MacDonald led Blackjack over to the side of the arena where the ringmaster was waiting for him. A blue ribbon was placed on Blackjack's headstall and then the photographer took their picture. As the photo was taken, the ringmaster handed out the remainder of the ribbons.

"Let's have one last look at our champions," boomed the voice of the announcer. The ring was now empty except for two horses. "Reserve is High Tree Go For It, owned by Mary Steele and shown by Fred Gilbert."

The Reserve Champion trotted out of the arena to the cheers of the crowd.

"And let's have a big round of applause for our Champion Futurity Three-Year-Old In-Hand winner, Gallant Image, owned by Chauncy Campbell and shown by Tom MacDonald."

Mr. MacDonald led the horse down the middle of the ring toward the out-gate at the far end of the arena. Everyone cheered enthusiastically, and

Heather couldn't believe how proud she was of the magnificent stallion. The photographer took one last picture of the horse as he strutted toward the gate.

The Futurity Driving Class was scheduled to go first during the Friday afternoon session, promptly at 1 p.m. When Heather and her mom arrived at the show grounds, the class had already started. Heather jumped out of the car before it came to a complete stop.

"I'll meet you at the arena, Mom!" she yelled as she hurried off.

By the time Heather got to the arena, the horses had gone the first way around the ring and were reversing direction. She quickly found Mr. MacDonald and asked him how Blackjack was doing.

"Chauncy is having a good drive today. Blackjack looks real nice. See, there he is."

Mr. MacDonald pointed to a horse at the far end of the arena. Heather looked at Blackjack, who once again looked absolutely gorgeous. But she didn't recognize Chauncy at first. He was all dressed up in a suit and was even wearing a hat. She'd never seen him in anything but old, beat-up blue jeans.

"Wow," she whispered to Mr. MacDonald. "They look great!"

Heather counted just eight horses in the class. "What happened to all the other horses, the ones that were in the in-hand class?" she asked Mr. MacDonald.

"Well, not all of them drive, and some of them are probably going in the park harness class instead. That's a class for horses that are more animated. They pick their feet up higher."

"I don't see how a horse could pick its feet up any higher than those out there!"

The class quickly came to an end, and all the horses lined up side by side down the center of the ring.

"Grooms in!" instructed the announcer.

Instantly eight people, including Mr. MacDonald, climbed through the rails and into the ring. Each one ran to a different horse and stood by it, waiting for the judge. When the judge approached Blackjack, Heather cheered. As she did so, she heard a familiar voice cheering beside her. She turned to see her mom smiling at her.

Once the judge had looked at every entry, he walked over to the corner of the ring, just to the left of Heather's group, opened a small gate, and disappeared into the judge's booth. Everyone relaxed while they waited for the results and, after a minute or so, the announcer's voice once again came over the speakers.

"We have the results for the Futurity Three-Year-Old Pleasure Driving class. The winner is number 86, High Tree Go For It, owned by Mary Steele and shown by Fred Gilbert."

Several people around Heather began to cheer, while Heather and her mom just looked at each other.

"It's okay," one of Mr. MacDonald's grooms reassured them. "You can't win them all, as long as—"

The announcer interrupted. "Second place goes to number 142, Gallant Image, owned and shown by Mr. Chauncy Campbell."

Everyone around Heather instantly started hollering their approval. Heather smiled and joined in.

Chauncy drove Blackjack to the center to collect their ribbon. The ringmaster pinned the long, flowing red ribbon to the headstall of Blackjack's bridle and gave the horse a friendly pat on the neck. Then Chauncy drove off and made his way to the out-gate.

"Come on, guys, let's meet them back at the barn!" one of the grooms suggested.

"I bet we can get there before they do!" another groom added, and they hurried off. Heather and her mom followed the girls back to the stalls.

"Where are they?" Heather asked once they had all returned to the stabling area.

"Here they come!" one of the grooms exclaimed, pointing off to the left.

Blackjack was approaching quickly, trotting high and proud, the red ribbon still attached to his bridle. As he got closer, Heather could see Chauncy and Mr. MacDonald riding together in the buggy, laughing and congratulating each other.

"Heather!" Chauncy said excitedly. "Good to see you. Did you see the whole class?"

"I missed the first few minutes, but I saw most of it. You two looked fantastic!"

"Thanks, it was a good drive. And it looks like we've got a shot at the championship. Just one more class to go!"

The high temperature for Saturday was expected to be 90 degrees; far too warm, thought Heather, to wear a wool saddle suit. To top it off, her class was scheduled for early afternoon, when the heat would be the worst.

When the Richardsons arrived at the fairgrounds, they immediately headed toward Mr. MacDonald's stalls. They found Chauncy and the trainer's grooms busily getting Blackjack ready.

"Heather!" Chauncy greeted her. "I'm glad you made it! I always get nervous that something is going to happen before one of our classes."

"Heather, darling, it's so nice to see you!" Heather and her parents turned around to see Mrs. Campbell approaching, carrying several cans of soda. "Okay, now who wanted what?" she asked as she started handing out soda. "I've got extras in case I missed somebody. Heather, would you like some soda?"

"No thanks, Mrs. Campbell. I don't think I could drink anything right now."

"Well if you're not going to have a soda dear, why don't you and your mom just follow me into the dressing room so that we can get started on your hair and makeup?"

Mrs. Campbell put down the drinks and motioned for Heather and her mom to follow her. They entered the dressing room, which was actually just another stall with curtains in front of it to provide some privacy. Inside the stall were a couple of chairs, a cot, and several hooks, upon which hung all sorts of shirts, pants, and ties. There was also a small table covered with several brushes, combs, hairnets, a hand mirror, and makeup.

"Sit here, dear," Mrs. Campbell said as she pointed to one of the chairs.

Heather sat down and forced a slight smile. "What are you going to do?" she asked sheepishly.

"Oh, not too much. Just make you look ten years older!" Mrs. Campbell joked. "Relax, honey, I've had lots of practice. You want to look professional."

Mrs. Richardson sat down in the other chair and quietly watched Chauncy's wife work. Within 15 minutes, Heather had been transformed into an older, more sophisticated-looking young woman. Mrs. Campbell handed Heather the hand mirror so that she could see the results.

"You look great, Heather," Mrs. Richardson encouraged her. "Although I don't think that's my daughter sitting next to me!"

"You guys almost done in there?" came Chauncy's voice. "They just called our class!"

The three women looked at each other in panic. "Here, Heather, put your suit on," Mrs. Campbell instructed as she handed Heather the saddle suit. "I've already attached your number to the back."

Heather hurriedly got dressed, and then made her grand entrance.

"Well, well," her dad said as he got his first look. "What do you think, Helen? That's not our little girl, is it?"

"Come on, Dad, stop teasing. Where's Blackjack?" Heather asked, suddenly realizing that she hadn't even had a chance to say hi to her beloved stallion.

"Here he is," Mr. MacDonald announced as he brought Blackjack out of the grooming stall.

Blackjack looked even more beautiful than before. His coat glistened, his polished feet shined, and his bright red patent leather headstall really made his head look gorgeous. The horse immediately saw Heather and nickered softly to her.

"Hi, Blackjack," Heather said quietly as she approached him and stroked his neck.

"Class 235, Futurity Three-Year-Old Pleasure, is about ten minutes away now. You should be making your way to the ring," came the loud voice over the speaker.

"Hop on, Heather," Chauncy instructed as he pulled the stirrups down on the saddle.

Once she was on the horse, Mrs. Campbell handed Heather her derby and gloves. Heather put them on, feeling the heat as soon as she did so. "Gosh it's hot up here," she mumbled.

As they walked to the ring, Heather felt like a princess with her entourage of friends. Once there, Mr. MacDonald's grooms set about cleaning the horse one last time, brushing here, cleaning there. One of them wiped a little trace of drool off the bit while another cleaned Heather's fancy boots with a towel.

"Remember to go easy on that right lead, now. Don't push him, and if he gives you any trouble—"

"Let's have one last look at Birchlane's Get a Life, the winner of class 234, Western Pleasure, Stallions and Geldings," blasted the speaker, drowning out Chauncy's instructions.

"Just relax and have fun." Chauncy smiled as he gave Blackjack one last pat. "And don't forget to breathe!"

"Good luck, honey!" cheered Heather's dad.

Heather gathered up her reins and looked around her. There were probably ten other horses, all quite beautiful and with far more experienced riders, she thought. At that, she started to panic. "Get a grip," she told herself. "You've got the most beautiful horse here, and we're going to show everybody how great he is!"

Feeling better, she urged Blackjack into a trot as the announcer called her class. The gate opened, and in stormed eleven horses, each one vying for the blue ribbon. As they entered the ring, the organist began playing a little medley whose beat matched the cadence of the horses' trots perfectly.

Blackjack felt good, thought Heather. His ears were forward, he was eager, and he was listening to his rider. Remembering one of Chauncy's instructions, she took a deep breath.

"Class is in order, all trot please. All trot," the announcer instructed. As Heather trotted down the rail, the show photographer took her picture. They continued to trot around the ring several times until the announcer asked everyone to walk. Heather brought Blackjack easily back to a walk and managed to catch a glance of the judge, who was looking right at her.

"All canter, please. All canter."

Blackjack picked up the canter effortlessly, but just as he took his first stride, a chestnut horse came running by him and pushed him toward the rail slightly. Caught off guard, Heather lost her balance and had to use her legs to keep herself on the horse. Somehow, Blackjack was able to overcome this sudden shift in his rider's weight, and continued to canter uninterrupted. Heather regained her balance and shot a nasty look at the chestnut horse, which was now in front of her, swishing its tail from side to side—a sure sign of irritation. As she passed the gate where her cheering section was, she heard Chauncy say, "You're doing great! Keep him going at that speed. That's perfect!"

The riders continued to canter their horses until they were instructed to walk. Within moments, they were asked to reverse and then, after just a short walk, the announcer asked for a trot. Blackjack once again broke into a trot, ears forward, happy to go. His trot seemed so airy and easy to ride that Heather felt she could go on forever. But then she had to bring her horse back to a walk, in anticipation of cantering. This time it would be on the right lead and she didn't know what Blackjack would do. He felt really good, but she had ridden him many times before when he had felt great and still given her trouble. As they walked around the ring, Heather began to get uptight, fearing for the worst.

"Canter, all canter," came the order.

Heather gave the signal to Blackjack, but instead of cantering, he pinned his ears and started to back up. "No, Blackjack, not now, not now," quietly pleaded his rider.

But Blackjack didn't listen to her, and took another step back. Heather tried to urge him on by using her legs, but she could feel her whole body tense up—and knew that Blackjack could feel it too.

Suddenly, the same horse who had run into them before came careening by them, so close that he almost ran into Blackjack again. Distracted by this sudden intrusion, Blackjack forgot about backing up. He pinned his ears back even further and his teeth flashed as he tried to bite the offender. He was unable to reach the other horse, but his forward momentum carried him into a canter in an effort to catch up to him.

Everything happened so quickly that Heather didn't have time to think, only to react.

"Good boy, keep going," she said, more to herself than her horse.

Within a few strides, the other horse was too far ahead of Blackjack to be any trouble. The chestnut's canter was more like an uncontrolled gallop, and as Heather watched, the horse passed almost everyone else, still swishing its tail. Meanwhile, Blackjack quickly settled down into his rocking horse canter. Knowing that the worst was behind her, Heather began to relax and actually managed to smile slightly.

After they'd cantered around the ring three times, the announcer told everyone to walk and then line up in the center of the ring. Heather brought her mount to the middle where the ringmaster was standing, both arms held out to show everyone where to stand. She tried to get to the end of the line so that she could be close to Chauncy and the others, but after she had stopped Blackjack and set him up in his show stretch, two other riders brought their horses between her and the gate. She glanced over toward her fans and could see them all smiling. Her mom, seeing that Heather was looking in her direction, started clapping while her dad gave her a thumbs-up. Chauncy and Mr. MacDonald were both wearing very big smiles. Heather smiled again

*Suddenly, the same horse who had run into them
before came careening by them.*

and patted Blackjack as he shook his head up and down several times, anxious to get going again.

Meanwhile, the judge was making his way down the line, getting his last look at everyone. After walking around each horse, he wrote down a few final numbers on his clipboard.

"You may retire your horses," the announcer instructed.

Heather looked around her and saw all of the horses walking to the far end of the arena, and followed them. The competitors clustered around the out-gate, many of them talking to friends or trainers standing at the rail. Heather sat there quietly, trying to relax.

"We have the results now for class 235, Futurity Three-Year-Old Pleasure."

Heather took a deep breath as the announcer paused. *Please, please, please,* she thought to herself.

"The winner of the class is number 89, Here's Looking at You, owned by Mr. and Mrs. Bill Cower and ridden by Mr. James Lockster."

Loud cheers of approval drowned out the announcer. A bay horse with a long, flowing tail who had been standing next to Heather turned around and trotted to the ringmaster. Heather watched the horse collect its ribbon.

"Hey, kiddo, you did great!"

Heather turned to see her dad leaning up against the rail. The whole group had made their way around the ring so that they could talk to her. She looked at Chauncy, who was still smiling.

"I'm sorry Chauncy, I didn't win," she said apologetically.

"Don't worry, you did great. Remember, I didn't say you had to win, just place. And even if you don't, who cares? You were able to get my horse into the ring and show him, and show him well. You should be really proud of yourself!"

"Second place goes to—"

Heather closed her eyes, trying to influence what the announcer would say next.

"—Number 41, Highlands Anchor, owned and ridden by Ms. Kathy Peters."

More cheers, this time from another section of onlookers. Heather opened her eyes and looked at the second place horse. The rider, a young woman, perhaps in her mid-twenties, hollered out, "Yes!" as she turned her horse toward the center of the ring.

"Hey Tom, the judge didn't see that little bobble at the canter, did he?" asked one of the grooms.

"I don't think so, he turned just as Blackjack started to break into a canter. At most, he could have marked the horse down for not getting into the canter soon enough. What do you think, Chauncy?"

"It didn't look like he saw—"

"Third place goes to 142, Gallant Image, owned by Mr. Chauncy Campbell and ridden by Ms. Heather Richardson."

Heather's mom screamed.

"You did it honey, you did it!" her dad congratulated her.

"What?" Heather asked, completely taken off guard by hearing her name called.

"Go get your ribbon," laughed Mr. MacDonald.

Snapping out of her fog, Heather turned Blackjack toward the ringmaster, and like those before her, collected a lovely ribbon. The ringmaster put the long yellow ribbon on Blackjack's bridle as he congratulated Heather.

"Thanks," she said shyly.

Then she turned her horse and proudly trotted out of the ring and over to where her parents and friends were waiting.

"We did it, we did it!" she exclaimed as she almost ran into Chauncy.

Everyone crowded around Blackjack, patting him and complimenting Heather.

"Do you think the judge saw it?" Heather asked.

"Saw what, honey?" her mom asked.

"Our screw up? When he wouldn't canter?"

"I don't think so, he was too busy watching another horse who started bucking," Mr. MacDonald explained.

"Really? I didn't see that."

"Well you were a little busy with your own horse," Chauncy laughed.

"Hey, Chauncy, who was the idiot riding the horse that kept running into me?"

"Oh, that was Jim Spencer, a trainer from up north. I use the term 'trainer' very lightly, since I wouldn't let him near any of my horses. He's very rough with his animals."

"What a jerk," Heather observed.

"Well, I think it's time to celebrate!" Mr. Richardson announced. "How about we all go out to dinner, my treat."

"All right!" cheered one of the grooms.

"Sounds good," Mrs. Campbell agreed. "Let's all get cleaned up, and then we can go out for an early dinner. That way we'll get back in plenty of time for the awards tonight."

Everyone returned to the stalls, got changed, and cleaned up quickly—except for Heather. She was too busy taking care of Blackjack. She cooled him off, brushed him, fed and watered him, and then just kept him company.

"Come on, honey, it's time to go," her dad said as he peered into the stall.

"I'll be ready in a minute," Heather replied. She gave the stallion one last kiss and then hurried off to change her clothes. Within five minutes, she was changed and headed off to the bathroom to wash up.

After dinner, the group made their way back to the show grounds to get Blackjack ready for the final presentation. There would be no judging, just all the futurity horses in the ring at the same time to see who would be champion.

"What do you think our chances are, Chauncy?" Mr. MacDonald asked.

"It's hard to tell. The Futurity has run for three years and I've lost track of who won what and when. But I think we've got a good shot at it. We're probably in the top three."

After half an hour of getting him ready, Mr. MacDonald led the black stallion to the arena, where they waited for the presentation.

Finally, the announcer started the evening session. "Welcome, ladies and gentlemen, to our final night of competition here at the Morgan Championship Show. Before we start our evening session, we'll be awarding the championship for the three-year-old futurity horses. Would all of the futurity horses please enter the ring?"

Twenty-one gorgeous horses trotted into the ring, led by their handlers in the same bridles that were used when they were shown in-hand.

"Please line up in the center of the ring," the announcer instructed.

The ringmaster made his way into the ring, carrying an enormous silver trophy and blanket, and patiently waited for the winner to be announced.

Heather clenched her fists and once again mumbled, "Please, please, please."

"This year's winner is number 142, Gallant Image, owned and bred by Mr. Chauncy Campbell!"

This time it was Heather who screamed. Chauncy jumped up in the air, cheering, and then quickly slipped through the gate. He ran over to his horse, who, by this time, had been led to the ringmaster to receive his award. The ringmaster put a blue sash around Blackjack's neck, an enormous blue, red, and yellow championship ribbon on his bridle, and held out the blanket, which was embroidered with the words "All Morgan Futurity Champion." Chauncy gave Tom MacDonald a big pat on the back as the photographer came over to take their picture.

"Wait a minute," Chauncy told the photographer.

He motioned to Heather, who looked at him, unsure of what he wanted.

"Get in here!" he yelled.

Heather, a puzzled look on her face, didn't move.

"Come on, Heather, get in here!" Chauncy repeated.

Most of the onlookers laughed, and Heather realized that Chauncy wanted her to join him in the winner's circle. A bit embarrassed, she cautiously climbed through the rails and ran to the center of the ring.

"Making the presentation this year is one of our Gold Ribbon Sponsors, Mr. James Hatcher."

Mr. Hatcher, a short, chunky man in a blue business suit, made his way into the ring. He took the trophy from the ringmaster and, with a big smile, posed next to the horse. Chauncy put his arm around Heather and told her to smile for the camera.

"A little closer to the horse, please," the photographer instructed. "There, that's good."

Heather looked at Blackjack with love and admiration, as the photographer took their picture.

TRAGEDY STRIKES

"**C**ome on, Heather, wake up, you're going to be late again!" a voice shouted from the kitchen.

"Oh no," groaned Heather. "I can't move." The alarm was blaring in her ear, so as usual, Heather threw the comforter over her head.

"Heather, I don't know how you can sleep with such a heavy comforter in June, but you've got to get going," her mother scolded as she came into the room, ripped the comforter away from Heather, and turned off the alarm. "Come on, breakfast is ready."

Heather groaned again and then lay in bed for a few minutes, forcing herself to wake up. She opened her eyes and stared at the long yellow ribbon that hung from her wall. Chauncy had given her the ribbon during one of the few quiet moments on Saturday night, while everyone was celebrating Blackjack's big win. He had said he was very proud of her and of all that she had achieved. Then he took her over to the far end of the fairgrounds, where the photographer had set up a booth. After looking over the photos, he'd ordered several 8 x 10 pictures of Blackjack. He ordered one of each class for himself, one of the championship for Mr. MacDonald, and two for Heather—one from her ride and one of the championship presentation. Then they walked back to the stables, where the celebratory party was in full swing.

Now it was back to reality. With only two weeks left of school, finals were just around the corner. Ugh. Exams. Studying left little time for anything else during the week. But she knew what she would be doing over the weekend.

On Saturday, Heather arrived at the barn bright and early. She hadn't seen Blackjack since the show, and was eager to take him on a trail ride without the pressure of an upcoming show. When she entered the barn, the horses all whinnied in anticipation of a treat.

"Hi, Rusty," she said as she handed him a carrot and gave him a pat. "Where's your neighbor?"

Looking over to Blackjack's stall, Heather was disappointed to see that her favorite horse was not sticking his head out to greet her. "Oh, there you are," she said, peering into the stall.

Blackjack was busy munching his hay, but he looked up when he heard Heather greet him. Although his coat had a healthy shine to it, the brilliant show gloss was missing, as was the black polish from his hooves.

"Back to my ol' puppy dog, huh?" Heather asked affectionately as she opened his stall door and put his halter on. "You know, I could have had some fancy outfit for my birthday, but instead I got you this halter. I hope you like it 'cause my mom sure thinks I'm nuts. Come on, let's go," she commanded as she led him out of the stall and up to the cross ties.

Chauncy had told her she could take the day off from cleaning stalls and just enjoy herself. Happy to do just that, Heather decided to go on a nice, long trail ride. She brushed her mount, tacked him up, and then led him outside. As she got on him, Chauncy walked up from the backfield.

"It's good to see you two together again."

"Yeah, it feels wonderful."

"Are you going for a trail ride?" Chauncy asked.

"Yup."

"Have fun. And if you get lost, be sure to come get me and I'll show you how to find your way back home!"

"Okay," she answered, before she really had a chance to think about what Chauncy had just said. "Wait a minute! How could I come and get you if I was lost?!"

Chauncy just chuckled and walked away. Heather smiled and then clucked to her horse as she guided him past the ring to the start of the trail. The trail was a large circle that started and ended at Chauncy's barn and had a wonderful assortment of terrains. It meandered through several sections of woods with varying degrees of overgrowth, interspersed with sections of open meadows and a few shallow brooks that crossed the trail. Every once in a while, they would come to a small pine tree grove where the sun had been shining on the fallen needles and pinesap. The aroma from this mixture of needles and resin was wonderful, a blend of woods and sun. And the weather was perfect—sunny but not too hot, with just enough of a breeze to keep most of the bugs away.

After riding for about an hour, Heather let her feet fall out of the stirrups and just enjoyed the scenery. It was such a wonderful day, and everything seemed to be going right. Blackjack plodded sleepily along, every once in a while nipping at a bug that had managed to find him. When they returned to the barn, Heather asked Chauncy if it would be okay for her to ride the following afternoon. Chauncy, of course, was more than happy to have her come over, although he warned her that he might be away. He was having a load of hay delivered in the morning and had promised his wife to take her out shopping afterwards.

"She always gets nervous when we get hay. She says she doesn't like to see me working so hard. It really isn't bad, since I have my son Dave come over and help me get the hay up into the loft. But to keep her happy I always promise to take her out afterwards," he explained.

The following afternoon, as Heather approached the barn, it became obvious that a load of hay had been delivered. There were individual pieces of hay all around the entrance to the barn—apparently where the hay had been taken off of a truck.

Inside the barn there was a path of hay leading to the overhead entrance to the hayloft. A hay conveyor rested against the hayloft door. It saved an enormous amount of work, since all you had to do was plug it in and it would take the bales of hay up to the loft. Heather thought it was rather strange that Chauncy hadn't bothered to put the hay conveyor away, since it took up most of the aisle and a horse could easily get hurt by it. She took a good long look at it and decided she could get Rusty past it if she was very careful.

Rusty was waiting for Heather, anxious to get out and play. She opened his stall door, put his halter on, and led him out. They made their way slowly around the hay conveyor, the horse cautiously sniffing it before agreeing to walk by it. As he passed it, though, one of his rear hoofs hit the metal and made a clanking noise, which startled both Heather and Rusty. The horse jumped forward slightly, pushing into Heather.

"Oww!" Heather exclaimed. "Could you be a little more careful, please?"

Heather had decided to take the same trail she had ridden with Blackjack the day before. Like the previous day, the weather was perfect and the ride was wonderful.

Once Rusty had been put back in his stall, she turned her attention to Blackjack. She brushed him, tacked him up, and headed to the ring. She really didn't want Blackjack to work hard; she just wanted to have fun, so she didn't take her riding too seriously. As they trotted along, she began to sing one of her favorite songs, which Blackjack really seemed to enjoy. The louder she sang, the higher Blackjack trotted, until he was trotting like the park horses whom she had seen at the show. She continued to sing throughout their ride, even as she gave the cue to canter on the right lead. Her mount, apparently enjoying the festive mood of his rider, immediately broke into a smooth canter. Heather laughed and congratulated the horse on his success.

After riding for a short while, she cooled Blackjack off and then put him away. She glanced at her watch; it was 4:30. She knew that Chauncy always fed his horses at 4:30 sharp, and it was unlike him to be late for a feeding, no matter what the reason. The horses were whinnying in the barn in anticipation of their dinner. Heather, having helped feed the horses many times, knew how much hay and grain each horse got, and so decided to do Chauncy a favor. After haying and graining the horses in the barn, she took a full bucket of grain out back to give to the pastured broodmares and their foals. They had been waiting near the gate, knowing that it was time for their dinner, too. Heather fed them and then returned to the tack room, where she left Chauncy a note on the small blackboard, saying, *I've fed all of the horses, see you tomorrow on the bus—Heather.*

Then she went up to the house, where she sat on the front steps and waited for her mother. Her mom arrived a few minutes later.

"Did you have fun? How was Blackjack? Did Chauncy get back in time to help you work him?" asked Mrs. Richardson as Heather got in the car.

"No, Chauncy isn't back yet. It's kinda weird 'cause he's never late. He makes sure the horses get fed at 4:30, no matter what. I decided to feed them for him."

Mrs. Richardson looked at her watch. "It's almost 5 o'clock. Well, I wouldn't worry too much. Mrs. Campbell is probably dragging him all over town!"

"Yeah, you're right. I just have a strange feeling."

Chauncy wasn't driving the bus the following morning. Heather, a bit concerned, asked the new driver if he knew anything.

"Nah, they just called me in this morning to cover for the regular guy," answered the young, greasy-looking driver.

That afternoon, there was a different driver covering for Chauncy.

"They told me he was out sick," answered the driver, an older woman wearing a baseball cap.

"Oh," was all Heather said.

Tuesday morning came, and still no Chauncy. The young, greasy-looking man was once again driving. Heather, intensely studying her math book, ignored him and sat in the back of the bus. By the end of the day, she was too exhausted from the stress of taking finals to worry about Chauncy. The math test had been tortuously hard, but she thought she had done okay on it. The English test hadn't been very hard—just long.

That night, Heather was in her room finishing up her industrial design project when the phone rang. She heard her mom run to the kitchen to answer it and didn't pay much attention to the conversation until she heard her mother say, "Oh no! I'm so sorry!"

Heather looked up from her bed, where she had been putting the finishing touches on a drawing of a house she had designed.

"Is he going to be okay?" her mother asked, pausing for a response. "Yes, I understand. Well that's good news, anyway."

Heather dropped her pencil and walked out to the kitchen, where she saw her mother talking on the phone, a very worried look on her face.

Another pause, this time much longer. "You're right, he shouldn't have done that."

"Mom, what's wrong, who is that?" asked Heather quietly.

Mrs. Richardson motioned to her daughter to be quiet. There was another pause while she listened to the caller, and then: "Yes, yes, we would. When? Oh, I understand, we'll wait then. Thanks so much for calling. We'll see you soon." And she hung up the phone.

"Mom, who was that? Is everything okay?" asked Heather softly.

"That was Mrs. Campbell on the phone and—"

"What happened to Chauncy?" Heather interrupted, panic in her voice.

"He's had a very serious heart attack."

Stunned by the news, Heather slowly backed up to the kitchen table and sat down. She started to feel very weak as her whole body began to tremble slightly.

"Is he going to die?" she asked, so shaken that she could hardly get the words out of her mouth.

"No, I don't think so," her mom said in a feeble attempt to reassure her. "The doctors think he will be okay, but it will take a long time and he'll have to take it very easy."

"How'd it happen, Mom?"

"Mrs. Campbell said that Chauncy and his son were putting hay up in the hayloft on Sunday. Just as they finished, Chauncy had the heart attack. It was probably the stress of putting all that hay away. I guess it was just too much for him."

"Oh my gosh, Mom, that means he must have had the heart attack right before we got there. That's why the hay conveyor was still in the barn."

Heather suddenly felt very guilty about enjoying Chauncy's horses on Sunday while he lay in a hospital.

"Mom? I'm scared."

"Me too, honey. Come on, let's say a prayer together."

Heather hated hospitals. When she was three years old she'd had to have her appendix removed, and it terrified her. She didn't remember much about the actual incident, just the terror and the antiseptic smell of the hospital. Now here she was again, but this time it was for a friend. As soon as she and her parents walked through the front doors of the hospital, the smell hit her. It was the same antiseptic odor that she remembered so well. Feeling very uncomfortable, she clung to her father.

They had had to wait until Chauncy was taken out of the ICU unit before they could visit.

"What's that?" Heather asked her dad.

"ICU means 'Intensive Care Unit,' Heather. That's where patients who are very sick stay."

They walked to the front desk, where the receptionist told them the best way to get to the third floor. Once there, they quickly found room 303 and walked quietly in. Still clinging to her father, Heather saw Chauncy asleep on the hospital bed, an IV tube running into his arm. Beside the bed, on a small table, was a cardiac monitor that beeped in rhythm to his beating heart. Standing next to the bed was Mrs. Campbell and a young man—probably one of Chauncy's children, Heather guessed.

"How's he doing?" asked Mr. Richardson.

"He seems to be doing better," the stranger answered. "Hi, I'm David Campbell. You must be Mr. Richardson."

"Hi, nice to meet you, David," said Mr. Richardson, holding out his hand.

Just then an older man in a white lab coat walked in. He was holding a clipboard, much like the judge at the horse show had. *But this was so far away from the show*, thought Heather.

"I've got good news for everyone. I have the results of Mr. Campbell's most recent EKG test, and it looks good. Considering that he had a major cardiac infarction, the test results are better than I expected. He'll have to stay here until he's passed through the acute phase that he's in now, but then I think we'll be able to move him into a rehabilitation program."

"What sort of a rehabilitation program, doctor?" Mrs. Campbell asked.

"A cardiac rehabilitation program. While in this program, we'll gradually increase the level of exercise that your husband gets. This will help rebuild the strength of his heart."

"How long does such a program last?" she continued.

"It really depends on the patient. It could run for just a few months, or much longer."

"How will we ever afford that?" a worried Mrs. Campbell asked her son. "Our insurance will never pay for all of this, it covers so little."

Mrs. Campbell looked as though she were about to cry.

"Don't worry, Mom, we'll think of a way. We always do," her son encouraged her, putting his arm around her.

At the sound of their voices, Chauncy opened his eyes. He looked over and saw Heather and her parents and smiled.

"Well hello there, young lady," he said weakly.

Heather tried to pretend nothing was wrong, but it didn't work. She was scared and it must have shown on her face. "Hi, Chauncy, how are you feeling?"

"I've been better," he joked.

Then Chauncy turned to his wife and son. Not wanting to upset him, they had dropped the conversation about the insurance.

"Hi, Dad," David said.

"Why are you still here? You've got a family to take care of."

"That's okay, Dad. Karen and the baby are staying with her parents for a few days. Don't worry."

Heather and her family stayed for about half an hour, making small talk and trying to look happy. Heather was sitting at a table over by the window with David, afraid to get too close to all the high-tech equipment near Chauncy. Eventually, a nurse came and told them that they would have to leave because Mr. Campbell needed to rest.

"You'll keep riding my horses for me, won't you Heather?" Chauncy asked as the Richardsons got ready to leave.

"Of course, Chauncy. Please don't worry; I'll make sure they are fine. Just hurry up and get better!"

The last day of school was supposed to be a very happy event. Everyone seemed to be overjoyed at the prospect of having the summer off. Everyone except Heather. She barely said a word all day, and just went through the motions. All she wanted to do was get home. Her parents had promised to take her to the farm the next day, and that was all she could think about. Mrs. Campbell had told them that her daughter Laura had come home to take care of the horses while her dad was in the hospital. Laura, she said, was a very competent horsewoman who had competed successfully with the family's horses until she moved away last year. She was attending college in a neighboring state and was working at the college for the summer, but had quickly quit her job when her dad had gotten ill.

When Heather arrived at the farm, there was no one there. She tacked up Blackjack and took him out for a trail ride along the same path that she had ridden the previous week with both Rusty and Blackjack. It was a gray, overcast day, and Heather's mood certainly matched the weather. Blackjack seemed to sense his rider's sadness, and carried his head lower than usual, plodding along like an old plow horse.

When Heather returned to the barn, a young woman was busy cleaning up the tack room. She was wearing old, worn blue jeans that had a hole in each knee, and a bright red shirt. In addition, she had shoulder-length blonde hair, bright blue eyes, and a pleasant, carefree look to her.

"Hi," said Heather said as she put Blackjack on the cross ties.

"Oh, hi," replied the woman as she turned around. "You must be Heather."

"Yeah, that's me." Heather smiled.

Blackjack seemed to sense his rider's sadness.

"I'm Laura Campbell. It's nice to meet you, Heather. I hear you've done quite a lot with Dad's horses."

Heather just nodded, too sad to say anything.

"I know Dad was thrilled when you started coming to the barn," Laura continued. "Because once I left, there was no one around to work them."

"How's Chauncy doing?" Heather asked.

"He's doing a little better, although I think the sale has really upset him."

"Sale? What sale?" Heather questioned, afraid to hear what was next.

"Didn't anyone tell you? Oh, gosh, I'm awfully sorry. I shouldn't really be the one to tell you."

"Please tell me," Heather said, desperation in her voice.

"Well, Dad's going to be in the hospital and in rehabilitation for a while. The only way we can pay for it is to sell the horses. I'm really sorry, I know how attached you are to them, but there's really no other way."

Heather's chest seemed to tighten as she tried to hold back the tears. All she could say, in a very feeble voice was, "All of them?"

"No, we're going to keep Rusty. Dad is so attached to him. We talked it over and decided it might be good for him to have one horse that he can take on buggy rides. You know, give him something to look forward to."

"Laura, are you there?" came a voice from outside the barn. "Come on, Mom's got lunch ready."

"I'll be there in a minute, Dave," Laura replied.

"When is the sale going to be?" Heather asked, a tear running down her cheek.

"Next Saturday at 10 a.m. Look, I'm so sorry to have to tell you this. I know how upsetting it is. I'm really upset, too. I've got such great memories of all these horses. But it has to be done; there's just no other way."

Laura walked over to Heather and gave her a hug. Feeling the tenderness of a stranger made it impossible for Heather to keep her feelings inside any longer. She burst into tears and started crying loudly. Laura continued to comfort her until Heather was able to collect herself a bit and the crying became sniffling.

"I'm so sorry, Heather. I'll leave you and the horses alone for a bit. Maybe that will help a little. I'll be up at the house. Why don't you come up when you feel better? Okay?"

Heather nodded 'yes' and then turned her attention to the black stallion. As soon as Laura had left, she buried her head in the young horse's mane and burst into tears again. Blackjack stood quietly, not moving a hoof. After a few minutes, Heather wiped the tears from her face and returned the horse to his stall. Unable to deal with losing her beloved horses, she decided to leave the barn. It was about time for her mom to come and pick her up, anyway.

As she walked toward the house, her mom drove in the driveway. Not wanting to face the Campbells right now, Heather ran to the car, opened the door, jumped in, and burst into tears.

THE AUCTION

O n the way home from the farm, Heather managed to tell her mother about the sale between bursts of crying. It was hard to get the words out because she felt as if her whole world was falling apart. Although she knew that in the past her parents had always been able to make her feel better, somehow she suspected that even they wouldn't be able to fix this problem.

"Maybe Dad will be able to think of something, honey."

"Like what, Mom?" sobbed Heather. "How could Dad ever help? I need to buy a whole farm full of horses and the barn to go with them! That'll never happen."

"I don't have an answer," replied Mrs. Richardson, taking her eye off the road for just a moment to look at her daughter. "I just think we should wait until we can talk to your father."

Heather didn't eat her lunch and barely touched her dinner. She spent the afternoon sulking in her room, thinking about all the fun she had had with Blackjack and Rusty, about all the things Chauncy

133

had promised to teach her this summer and about how she was going to miss her beloved horses. She also thought about who might buy the horses. Perhaps someone who did not have the patience or understanding to work with Blackjack might take him home, and destroy all the hard work that Heather had put into him. How could anyone else understand his little peculiarities, how you needed to talk to him while riding, how he loved to have his ears scratched and rest his head on a nearby shoulder? What about the broodmares? Queen and Lady and the others? Chauncy had worked for years to acquire just the right horses, and now that he seemed to have collected and bred the best around, they were going to be sold.

Finally, Mr. Richardson came home. "Hey, hon, how was your day?"

"Well, John, we've got a problem," began Mrs. Richardson. "It seems that in order to pay the insurance bills, the Campbells have decided to have an auction and sell all of Chauncy's horses, with the exception of Rusty."

"Dad?" Heather asked.

"Yes?"

"What can I do? I can't imagine not having the horses around. I really love them."

"I know you do, Heather."

"Dad, I feel lost."

"Well, let me think," replied her father. "There has to be something we can do. What about the place where you took lessons last year? Maybe we could lease one of their school horses?"

"That's not the same, Dad. Chauncy's horses are special. It's really hard to explain to someone who has never been around horses much, but when I ride Blackjack, I really feel a special bond with him. He's my best friend and I..."

Heather started to cry again. Her father reached over and gave her a big bear hug.

"Okay, honey, don't cry," he encouraged, as he continued to hug her. "We'll think of something. Come on now, let's not cry, okay?" he said, as sympathetically as possible.

"I'll try, Dad, but it's hard."

Mr. Richardson got quiet as he tried to think of a solution to his daughter's dilemma. He walked over to the kitchen table, sat down, and loosened his tie. With both elbows on the table, he raised his hands to support his chin as he silently searched for an answer.

"How much money do you have in your savings account, Heather?"

"About $300, Dad, but that's not enough to buy Blackjack."

"You're right, Heather. I don't think that will be enough to buy your horse."

"What can we do?" pleaded Heather.

"Wellllll," said her father, dragging out the word for effect, "how about if I loan you another $700 so that you have $1000? Will that help?"

"It might, but I really don't know how much he'll sell for, plus where would I keep him?"

"You'll have to spend some time this week looking for a place to board him. I'm willing to pay for his board. As for the loan, we can work out the details later but you'll have to pay back a little each month. After all, he will be your horse. As for how much Blackjack will sell for, maybe he won't sell for much. Let's think positive."

"Okay, Dad, I'll start calling places tomorrow."

She led Blackjack down the aisle toward the sliding doors. She tried to open them, but just like the first time when she was trying to get in, they moved an inch or so and then stopped. She looked down and saw a lock on the floor that was keeping the doors from opening. Without thinking, she bent down and unlatched it. As soon as she did this a loud, blaring alarm went off.

"Oh no, we're trapped! It's the alarm, the alarm, the alarm!"

Knowing that she would soon be caught, she decided to open the sliding doors and make a run for it. But as she pushed one of the heavy doors to the side, her horse panicked and began to back up.

Turning to face the animal, she pleaded with him to follow her out of the barn. "Come on, we've got to get out of here, now!" But it was no use; the horse continued to slowly back up, away from the doors.

"Thought you'd take my horse, did you?"

Turning, the girl saw a tall, dark-clothed man whose face she couldn't make out.

"You'll never get my horse!" she shouted angrily.

"Wanna bet?" came the nasty reply. "He's *my* horse now. Besides, the police are on their way. They'll be here any minute."

"Come on, let's get going," came another voice— *perhaps the police*, thought the girl.

"Come on, let's get going," came the voice again. "Wake up, Heather, you've already wasted half the morning sleeping!"

Heather opened her eyes and saw her mother standing over her. "Uhh," she sighed, very relieved, although her heart continued to beat at a frightening pace. "It was just a dream."

"Come on, Heather, I thought you were going to make a bunch of calls this morning to try and find a place to board Blackjack! If you still want me to drive you to any of them, then we've got to get going soon."

"Sorry, Mom, I didn't mean to sleep so late."

Heather lay in bed for a few minutes after her mom left her room. Knowing that in the past, her dreams had somehow foretold bits and pieces of her future with Blackjack, she was worried now that Blackjack might be in trouble. Maybe her dream meant her horse was going to be bought by some cruel man who might hurt the beautiful animal. It couldn't be just a coincidence that the dream had returned.

She got up, dressed, grabbed her phone and then walked out to the kitchen. Sitting down at the table, she began a search on her phone for 'Local Horses.'

"Nothing," she muttered.

"How about 'Boarding Facilities'?"

Heather typed in the new words and waited a moment before saying, "Nope, just dog and cat boarding."

"Try 'Riding,' then," her mother suggested.

Heather again typed what her mother suggested. "Oh, here's something. No, that one won't work. Let's see ... ummm, no. Maybe this one? Hey, Mom, I found something. It says they offer 'riding instruction'."

"Give it a try. The worst that can happen is that they say they don't board."

"Okay," Heather replied as she touched the number on the screen. "Hello?" she asked when someone answered the phone. "I'm calling to see if you board horses. You do? Great!"

"Ask them how much!" her mother whispered.

"Oh, how much do you charge? Wow, that much? No, no. I didn't realize that was the going price.

Okay, yeah, I understand. Can we come out and look? Great. In about an hour? Okay. By the way, my horse is a stallion. Does that matter? Oh. But he's really good and ..." Heather paused as she listened to a long explanation. "Okay, yeah, I understand, thank you."

"What did they say?" asked Mrs. Richardson.

"They don't accept stallions and they said they didn't know anyone who would."

"Why not?" asked her confused mother.

"Because they can be unpredictable. You can't pasture stallions with other horses, and some people just don't like dealing with them."

"Well, keep calling, honey. Somebody must be willing to board stallions."

Heather made five more calls, but each conversation went pretty much like the first one. The person on the other end of the phone was very willing to take a new boarder until he found out that the new resident would be a stallion. Nobody wanted a stallion. By the sixth call, Heather just told the person that she was looking for a place to board a stallion right away.

"Nope, sorry, we don't take stallions," came the expected response.

"Okay, thank you," sighed Heather, and then, in a last-ditch effort: "Do you know anyone who might? He's really gentle and well-behaved."

"Try Stream Lake Horses. I think they might take them. I don't know their phone number, but you can look them up. They're in Coolridge."

"Thank you," Heather said. Turning to her mom, she said, "That's it. There aren't any more listings. But that last guy gave me the name of a place in Coolridge."

"Coolridge is kind of far."

"What else can I do, Mom?" Heather asked, somewhat flustered by the situation.

"I guess you've got to call."

When Heather called, she was delighted to find that they did, in fact, accept stallions. Getting directions, she made an appointment in one hour.

Mrs. Richardson went into her bedroom to grab her purse and car keys, and off they went.

They arrived at Stream Lake Horses with five minutes to spare.

"Yuck," Heather said quietly as she got out of the car. "Mom, this place is gross."

The whole facility looked like a tornado had just come through and only left the junk behind.

"I agree. I think we should leave."

"Hello there!" a sprightly man greeted them, walking toward them from the dilapidated barn that stood before them. "You must be Heather Richardson."

"Uh huh," Heather replied, staring at the barn, which looked like it was about to fall over at any moment.

"I'm Nick Casper. Come on in, I'll show you around."

Heather and her mom, unable to get away, followed their tour guide toward the barn. Mr. Casper wore ragged jeans and a faded blue shirt that showed off his well-toned arms. He had a full head of dark brown hair, deep blue eyes, and a kind look to his face. Heather guessed that he was probably around 30 years old. The barn that they were about to enter, however, did not have a kindly look. It was a very old, decrepit looking thing. Most of the white paint on the outside had chipped away, with only a few spots here and there remaining. The grounds around the barn were not much better. There were old, rusted parts of cars and tractors all over the place, as well as numerous boards, several with nails sticking out of them.

As they entered the barn, Heather could instantly see that the inside was not much better. It was dark and there was a strong smell of something musty. It reminded her of an old, moldy bale of hay that Chauncy had shown her once—hay that he explained should never be fed to horses. There were ten stalls in the barn, and an overhead loft that appeared to be filled with hay. Only three of the stalls had horses in them, and although the stalls were large, they were also dirty, full of old bedding that needed to be changed. As Heather peered into one of the empty stalls, still filthy from its previous tenant, she smelled a new odor: the overpowering stench of ammonia, caused by urine-soaked bedding. It hurt her eyes. She could never imagine Blackjack living in such a place.

As they walked by one of the occupied stalls, Heather saw a horse pawing at the dirty bedding, looking for food. "Hi," Heather said as she reached into the stall to pct the horse.

The animal, a small buckskin mare, stopped her pawing and walked over to Heather. She was friendly and relatively clean, except for the manure that covered her back legs. The mare let Heather scratch her for a brief moment and then walked away and continued her pawing.

As the tour progressed, Heather pretended to listen to Mr. Casper as he talked about his facility, but since she knew that she would never keep a horse here, she ignored him. Her mother, however, listened intently and continuously said "Oh," "Uh huh," and "Really?"

"So that's about it," said Mr. Casper. "I think you've seen just about everything."

"Okay. Well, honey, do you have any questions for Mr. Casper?"

"No, Mom, I think he's answered all my questions."

"Okay then. Thank you very much, Mr. Casper," Mrs. Richardson said as she reached out and shook the man's hand. "My daughter and I need to talk it over. I'll be in touch."

With that, the mother and daughter turned and left. As they got in the car, Heather asked, "Geeze, Mom, how could you be so nice? That place was revolting!"

"I know. But I have a hard time looking someone in the face and telling him that his place is disgusting. I think I'm just too polite."

Mrs. Richardson started the car, pulled out of the driveway, and drove away as the two of them continued to talk.

"I guess so. You know that there's no way I could ever keep Blackjack there."

"Of course. Besides, I'd never let you hang around such a place."

"So now what?"

"We keep looking."

Heather and her mom searched all week, but they quickly exhausted all possibilities. Finally, in desperation, Mrs. Richardson called Mrs. Campbell on Friday. Mrs. Campbell agreed that, should Heather buy Blackjack, she could keep him at the farm until a good place to board him could be found.

143

Saturday morning dawned bright and warm—a good day to go to the beach, Heather's mother said at breakfast. Of course, Mrs. Richardson knew that they would be spending the morning at Chauncy's in an attempt to buy Blackjack. She had been trying to cheer Heather up, but her attempts were failing miserably.

That morning, when they approached Mill Creek Road, they saw a large white sign that said "Morgan Horse Sale" in bright red letters, with a huge arrow pointing toward the farm. Well before they could see the property, they noticed cars and trucks with trailers attached parked along both sides of the road.

"Wow, there must be tons of people here," Heather remarked as Mr. Richardson drove the car past the farm so that he could find a parking place. They drove beyond the next two houses before they found a spot large enough for the car. Once parked, the Richardsons got out of the car and walked silently toward the farm.

At the barn, they were amazed to see so many people milling about. "There must be a hundred people here," Heather muttered.

"Probably more," guessed her mother.

"Oh, look at these," her father said, trying to distract them. He had picked up a sales catalog from a pile on a table between some photos of the horses. He handed one to his daughter, who quickly began to leaf through the papers. It was a small, photocopied booklet, obviously put together in a hurry.

On each page was a photo of a horse. Below the photo was the horse's name as well as the names of both of its parents. Then there was a brief description of the horse.

Heather quickly thumbed through the catalog, looking for Blackjack's photo. She found it at the end of the book.

"Does that mean he's going last?" she asked.

"Looks like it."

"Then even if he goes for too much money, I can't buy one of the other horses, Dad. I won't know until it's too late."

"That does cause a problem, doesn't it? I wasn't planning on that."

Feeling as though everything was lost, Heather decided to go into the barn and see Blackjack. But when she looked up from the catalog toward the barn, she realized that getting into the barn would be extremely difficult. It was packed with people, all of them staring into stalls or poking at the horses. She really wanted to see her horse, just to let him know that she was here and to hopefully give him a big hug. She especially needed to feel his hot breath on her face one more time, and hide her face in his long, flowing mane. As she squeezed between two people so that she could see better, a bell rang.

"May I have your attention please!" came a man's voice from the outdoor ring. "The sale will be starting in five minutes. Would you take your seats, please?"

People around Heather started to turn toward the voice.

"Mom?"

"I'm right behind you, Heather," Mrs. Richardson said as she grabbed Heather's shoulder. "Come on, honey, let's try and get a good seat."

They slowly followed the crowd toward the ring. The gate was tied open, and inside the ring were about fifty metal chairs set up in rows. Heather wanted to get near the front, and since most people seemed reluctant to be seen there, they were able to get three seats in the second row. Heather sat between her parents and silently fumbled with her sales catalog, quickly looking through it, then putting it down in her lap, then picking it up again. After what seemed like an eternity, everyone was seated.

Heather felt her palms getting sweaty, and her heart began to race a little. She turned around to see if any of the horses were coming in, but all she could see were the faces of strangers. Most of the chairs were taken and quite a few people were standing up at the back and along the outside of the ring. Then a gentleman dressed in a business suit ambled toward a podium that had been set up outside the ring, right near the fence where the horses would stand. He tapped the microphone, which made a loud, screeching noise.

"Testing, testing. Okay, can you hear me back there?"

"Yeah."

"Yes."

"We can always hear you, Dave!" someone shouted from the back of the audience.

"Well, then, let's get started. My name is Dave Kingly and I'd like to welcome everyone here today to the dispersal sale of Gallant Morgans. As most of you probably know, Mr. Chauncy Campbell suffered a severe heart attack a few weeks ago, and although he's expected to make a full recovery, his family has decided to disperse his herd. First off, I'd like to send our wishes to Chauncy for a speedy recovery. I hear he's already driving all the nurses crazy with his Yankee humor."

Many people in the audience chuckled, most likely those who knew Chauncy well enough to understand his sense of humor.

"As anyone who is familiar with Morgans in New England knows, Mr. Campbell assembled quite a nice herd of horses. It took him years to achieve his goals, and what you will see here today are the results. So let's bring out lot number one. Bill? Are you ready?"

After a moment of silence, murmurs were heard from the back of the crowd as another gentleman in a business suit led a bay mare past the chairs to the front of the ring. As the mare trotted toward the front, she gave a loud whinny. A soft, high-pitched whinny answered as a small bay filly came running toward its mother. Queen was wearing a leather halter and kept tossing her head high into the air. Her handler was trying to get her to stand still and stretch out in a show pose, but she refused. Instead, she pranced around and continued to whinny. Her filly, confused and frightened by all the commotion, tried to stay as close to her mother as she could.

"Lot number one is Gallant Queen, a 12-year-old bay mare and her weanling filly, Gallant Vista. Gallant Queen is by Windstream Omega and out of Gallant Mabel. Mabel was the first Morgan to carry the Gallant prefix. Queen's filly, Vista, is by Starfleet Lead On, one of today's leading sires. Okay, who'll start the bidding at $2000? Do I hear $2000?"

There was no answer. "How about $1000! Do I hear $1000?" Still no answer.

"Come on folks, this is a quality mare. Don't miss out on a chance to buy a great horse. Do I hear $800?"

Heather grew even more uncomfortable in her chair. Should she bid on Queen? She had enough money, and she knew that once the foal was weaned, Queen would make a nice riding horse. But if she bid, then she couldn't bid on Blackjack.

"Dad," she whispered to her father, "why isn't anyone bidding?"

"A lot of times the first lot in an auction doesn't sell for very much. It takes a few minutes for people to get into the action and—"

"Yes!" came a shout from the back.

Heather turned to see yet another well-dressed man standing near the last row of chairs. He was pointing at a woman in a very bright red dress who was nodding and smiling. Heather then noticed that there were two other well-clothed men who were walking around the audience; apparently they were there to help the auctioneer.

"We have $800, do I hear $1000?"

"Yes! We have it here!" announced another voice. "A bid for $1000. Do I hear $1200?"

"I'll bid $1200!" came the first voice. The woman in the red dress obviously wanted Queen.

Heather felt a strange feeling of relief because, although she wanted Queen, the decision was now out of her hands. She didn't have enough money to buy her, and could now just sit and watch. But if Queen was going for more than $1000, what would Blackjack go for?

"How about $1500? Do I hear $1500?"

There was a moment of silence as the second bidder tried to decide if he wanted to bid more.

"I'll do $1400," said the second bidder quietly.

"Yes! We have $1400. Do I hear $1500?" asked the auctioneer.

"Yes!" declared the first gentleman—just as Queen let out a loud whinny.

"I have $1500. Do I hear $1600? How about $1600?" continued the auctioneer. But the second bidder did not want to bid any more.

"Just $1500? Going once, twice, sold!" he hollered as he slammed his gavel down on the podium. "Ken? Would you get our lucky bidder's name please?"

There was a pause as the assistant asked the bidder's name. Then he repeated it so that everyone could hear. "Susan Wentworth of Coolridge."

The auctioneer picked up a pen that had been on the podium and scribbled something down on a pad of paper as Queen and her foal were led away.

"Okay, now let's really get going. Lot number two is fabulous. Gallant Lady and her weanling colt, Gallant Expedition. Bill, would you bring them in please?"

The auction continued for an hour. All of Chauncy's prized horses went through the sale, going off to strange new homes. None of the animals sold for less than $1000. In fact, the lowest-selling horse sold for $1200. Most of the other horses sold for much more. By the time the auctioneer asked for the final lot, Heather had chewed several fingernails ragged.

"Okay, folks! Now I know you've really been waiting for our final lot, Gallant Image. Bill, bring him in!"

The crowd turned to look toward the barn. Within a few moments, most of those in attendance were making hushed comments. Many of these commentaries were too muffled for Heather to hear, but she was able to make out several, which included, "Oh my gosh," "He's gorgeous," and "That's the one you want, isn't it dear?"

Heather started to squirm even more in her seat as she strained to see Blackjack make his entrance. Finally, in desperation, she stood up. Still unable to see, she climbed onto her seat and balanced herself by holding onto her dad with one hand. By doing this she was able to see the tops of Blackjack's ears, and then his head, his neck, and finally the rest of his body. The horse gave out a loud, deep whinny, much more masculine than the ones Queen had vocalized. The stallion was led past the crowd, snorting and prancing all the way. He looked beautiful. He was wearing his fancy show bridle, the one he had worn during the in-hand class at the Morgan show, and his coat glistened with the sheen that Heather had seen only during his appearance at the Futurity. The horse knew that everyone was looking at him, and, thinking that he was at a show, he wanted all those strangers to see just how special he was. His handler seemed a bit concerned at the antics of the stallion, but Heather knew that it was all just an act.

She smiled at Blackjack and felt a tinge of pride as the audience admired the horse that she had taken care of just a few weeks earlier.

"Our final lot is Gallant Image," began the auctioneer. "He is by Imagine That and out of Gallant Queen, who sold in this sale. This horse, at just three years of age, already has a spectacular show record, having won the Futurity Grand Championship at the Morgan Regional Show just a short while ago. He has been shown in-hand, in harness, and under saddle, and I'm even told that he has been ridden on the trails. If you look at his breeding, you can see what a great future he'll have in the breeding shed. Go ahead folks, take a peek at his great bloodlines. It's right there in the sales catalog."

Heather could hear papers being shuffled as many in the crowd opened their catalogs to see just what was so great about this horse.

"Look at him, folks. Isn't he beautiful?"

Blackjack was now in front of the crowd, posing in a show stretch that his handler had requested. He turned his head to look at the crowd, and the red patent leather browband radiated in the sun as he gave out another loud whinny.

"Now you know folks, if you buy this horse you won't be throwing your money away! He is an investment that will return your money many times! Just think of all the beautiful foals he'll produce, and the enjoyment you'll have showing him. You know that his show career is just beginning. He's got many years of great victory passes left in him! Okay, now who'll start the bidding at $5000?"

"Our final lot is Gallant Image."

Heather's eyes popped open.

"What?" she whispered to her father, "They can't do that, can they?"

"They can start the bidding at whatever they want."

"But Dad, how can I—"

"Yes!" hollered one of the assistants from the back. "We have $5000!"

"Dad?"

Mr. Richardson put his left arm around Heather's shoulder and held her hands in his right hand. As the bidding continued at a furious pace, the voice of the auctioneer faded away. Tears streamed down Heather's face and her mind drifted off to all the happy days she had shared with Blackjack. Suddenly she was riding her favorite Morgan bareback through the pine grove where the scent of fallen needles filled the air. A bright red cardinal sang its peaceful song from the branches overhead as a deer-fly landed on the horse's neck. She swatted the fly, and the tranquil picture was instantly destroyed by the pounding of the auctioneer's gavel.

"Sold! A price of $18,000 for a great horse. Ken, what's the name of the bidder please?"

"Mr. Tom MacDonald for a client."

"Well then, sold to a client of Mr. MacDonald's. There's a man who knows his horses folks!" As Blackjack was led back to his stall, the auctioneer finished up with his duties. "I'd like to thank you all for coming here today, and congratulate everyone who successfully bid. If those of you who bought horses would make your way up to the house, where we can settle your accounts, we'd appreciate it. Thanks again, everyone."

Mr. Kingly shut off the microphone and walked away from the podium. Most of the people in the audience were already standing up and trying to make their way out of the ring, but Heather and her parents didn't move. Mr. and Mrs. Richardson sat silently while their daughter just stared into space, tears slowly falling down her cheeks.

Finally, after about five minutes, Heather announced, "Let's get out of here. I want to go home."

"Okay, honey," agreed her father. "Why don't we go grab some lunch?"

"No. I want to go home. I just want to go home," she pleaded quietly as she got up and walked away.

As Heather made her way past the barn, she heard a man's voice call her name. The voice sounded familiar, but she couldn't quite place it. She turned in the direction of the barn and saw Mr. MacDonald coming toward her.

"Heather, I'm glad I saw you."

"Hi, Mr. MacDonald," she said in a hushed voice.

"I just wanted to let you know that Blackjack is in good hands. I know how much he means to you, and I don't want you to worry."

By this time, Heather's parents had caught up with her and were standing on either side of their daughter. After greeting her parents, the trainer continued, "I bought him for a client who plans to keep him in training with me."

"Is he here?" Heather asked.

"No, he's away on a business trip. He travels a lot. In fact, I've only seen him in person twice. But he seems like a nice man."

"Look out! Coming through!" a man yelled, leading Lady past the lingering crowd. Two other men were trying desperately to get her foal to follow. Heather watched as they forced the foal along, over the grass and to the road, where a trailer waited to take them to a new home. She grabbed her dad's arm with both hands as she stared at Lady for the last time. As they disappeared from view, her attention returned to Mr. MacDonald.

"Anyway, I wanted to tell you that you'd be welcome to visit any time. Okay?" He looked Heather right in the eyes. "Promise you'll come if you get the chance?"

"I promise, Mr. MacDonald."

Heather knew that it would be very unlikely. Mr. MacDonald lived a full two hours away, and she didn't think she'd ever be able to convince her mom to drive four hours roundtrip just to visit a horse. She peered into the barn to try to see Blackjack, because she really wanted to say goodbye to her beloved horse. But when she saw the huge crowd of people around his stall, she knew it was impossible. Besides, she certainly didn't want to start crying in front of all of them.

"Mom? Dad? Can we go now?"

"Sure," her mom said. She and her husband shook Mr. MacDonald's hand and said their goodbyes.

By the time the Richardsons got home, it was so hot out that Mr. Richardson went straight for the air conditioner and turned it on high. Mrs. Richardson started going through the mail while Heather quietly got a drink of water. "Heather?"

"Yeah, Mom?"

"Here's something for you," her mother said. She handed her daughter a large manila envelope. Heather didn't know what the package contained, and opened it carefully. Inside were two beautiful photos. The first showed Heather riding Blackjack during their class at the Morgan Show. Heather was stunned; she had completely forgotten about the photos that Chauncy had ordered. She then pulled the second photo out of the envelope and saw a dream from the past. There was Chauncy, the picture of health, with his arm around Heather and a big smile on his face. And there she was, a huge smile on her face as well, looking at the horse she loved so much. It seemed like so long ago, and yet it had only been a few short weeks. Heather dropped the photos and ran to her room.

BLACKJACK'S TERROR

Heather spent the next few days in what her mother referred to as a trance. She did not leave the house, and most of the time she stayed in her room listening to music.

Heather shed a lot of tears thinking about all the things that might have been. Chauncy was going to teach her how to work with the foals, and then there were going to be all those wonderful, long trail rides with Blackjack. But now that was gone. The mares and foals had all been taken to new homes, and Heather would probably never see them again. And Blackjack was with a new trainer. Mr. MacDonald was a very nice man, and Chauncy had complete faith in his training abilities, but would he be able to work through the cantering problem like she had? Would he have the patience that it required, or would his client, Blackjack's new owner, insist that time not be wasted on such foolishness? Would Blackjack rebel against new training methods and get even worse? The more she thought about it, the more upset she became. She had decided to stay away from everything even remotely connected to horses; it hurt too much.

The next morning, she was awakened by her father. "What are you doing here, Dad? Don't you have to work today?" she asked sleepily.

"I took the day off. Come on, get out of bed. We've got a busy day planned."

Heather knew that something was up. Annoyed at her father for getting involved, she was still somewhat relieved to be able to spend some time alone with him. He had always been easy to talk to, and seemed to understand how she felt.

"Where are we going?" she asked after showering, getting dressed, and having breakfast.

"That's for me to know and you to find out," he replied in a mischievous voice. "Come on, let's go!"

With that, he led his daughter to the car. She climbed in and Mr. Richardson started driving, and it wasn't long before she realized that they were driving to Chauncy's farm.

"Dad, I really don't want to go to the farm."

"I know, but you're going to, so give it up. You're not going to get me to turn around."

"But I really don't want to go. I don't think I can stand seeing all those empty stalls." She hesitated. "Especially Blackjack's."

"Relax, Heather. You are going to have fun today and that's an order," he said playfully.

When they arrived at the farm, Heather got out of the car and obediently followed her dad to the barn. Rusty was standing in front of the barn, already hooked to Chauncy's show buggy, with Laura Campbell patiently holding him.

"Surprise!" Laura called as the two visitors came into view. As they approached, Rusty turned his head and nickered softly.

Heather cautiously walked over to Rusty. She felt like she would be betraying herself and Blackjack if she just acted as though nothing was wrong. She stopped just out of petting range of the horse. She knew her dad and Laura were watching her, but right now all she wanted to do was run away. Rusty, still looking at her, nickered again. Reluctantly, she walked over to him. The horse raised his muzzle up to Heather's face and stared at her. Suddenly, any feelings of staying away melted as she felt Rusty's warm breath blow in her face.

"Hi, big guy," she said affectionately as she stroked the horse's neck. "I forgot how much I missed you."

The buggy ride was wonderful. At first Heather was somewhat quiet, thinking once again about Blackjack and all that could have been. But as they drove along, the fresh scent of the pine trees, the clopping of Rusty's shoes, and her dad's companionship cheered her up. They continued down the road for about an hour, mostly walking, but every once in a while Heather would ask Rusty to trot. Rusty, happy to be out, would raise his whole body up from the relaxed position he used while walking and eagerly trot along until he was told to stop. Meanwhile, Heather and her dad talked about everything and anything. They talked about Chauncy and his prognosis, the horses, Mr. Richardson's job, Mrs. Richardson's obsession with buying so many pairs of shoes, Heather's future plans, and her plans for the rest of the summer.

After a lot of thought and discussion, Heather finally agreed that it would be best if she continued to work with Rusty. She knew that it would be hard, but she also realized, with the help of her dad, that it wasn't fair to Rusty for her to just disappear. He needed exercise and, as was apparent, also really wanted the attention. In addition, Chauncy would hopefully be home by fall, and it would be best if his horse had been regularly worked before he started to drive him.

"Good, then it's settled!" announced Mr. Richardson. "Now how about a big, juicy mushroom burger? I'm starving!"

The two companions looked at each other and laughed. When they returned to the barn it was almost lunchtime. Heather released the harness hooks from the buggy while her dad held the horse. Then she removed the harness from Rusty and put it away in the tack room. She groomed the patient bay gelding and led him back to his stall. It was strange being in the barn now that it was so empty, and Heather glanced over at Blackjack's stall as she closed Rusty's door, but quickly looked away. It hurt too much to see it empty. She reached down to a bale of hay that was leaning against the wall, grabbed a flake, and tossed it to Rusty.

Once the horse was put away, Heather and her dad made their way to the house to thank Laura.

"I had a really good time, Laura. Thanks for forcing me to come out here and letting me drive Rusty," Heather said when Laura answered the door.

"Great! That means you'll be back, right?"

"Yeah, how about tomorrow?"

"Sure, you can come any time. Rusty loves the attention."

"I noticed! Thanks again," said Heather as she turned to leave.

After a big lunch, Mr. Richardson took his daughter to visit Chauncy. He had just been moved from the hospital to a special rehabilitation center, where he was to spend a month or so getting his strength back. It took an hour to get there, but it was worth it just to see the smile on Chauncy's face as Heather walked into his room.

"Hi, Chauncy! Surprise!" Heather greeted him.

"Heather, I'm so glad you could come," Chauncy said. He was sitting at a small table, dressed in his work clothes, reading a newspaper. "I've been so bored. All I want to do is get out of here, but they won't let me."

"Seems to me you should enjoy all the pampering," Mr. Richardson stated as he walked into the room.

"Nah, after a day or so it gets pretty tedious." Anxious to end the small talk and discuss his favorite subject, Chauncy asked, "How is Rusty, Heather? Have you been down to the farm to see him?"

"We went to the farm this morning and took Rusty out for a drive."

"You drove Rusty?"

"Yeah, it was fun and Rusty really seemed to enjoy it."

"That's good. Now I want you to keep working Rusty, because I expect him to be all tuned up for me when I get out of this blasted place."

"When do you expect to be released?" Mr. Richardson asked.

"I don't know for sure, maybe the start of August, or even the end of July. Nobody around here seems to want to give me any straight answers. I guess it depends on how quickly I get my strength back. We've got enough money now, since the insurance came through with more than we expected and we got so much from the auction." Chauncy's voice drifted off. He paused, staring at the wall, and then turned back to Heather. "I'm so sorry about what we had to do, Heather, and I know how you must feel because I feel it too. But my family really had no choice. We couldn't afford to feed all those horses this winter, nor could I take care of so many

164

animals. I'm afraid one is all I can handle right now. Especially if I'm supposed to be taking it easy."

Heather's tumultuous emotions came storming back. Suddenly she felt as though she were going to cry. Holding back her tears, she managed to say, "I know you had to do it, Chauncy, because there's no way you'd ever sell Blackjack unless you really had to. It was hard watching all the horses get sold to strangers, but I know you had no other choice."

"You're right. If it makes you feel any better, I've talked to Tom, and he's really excited about having Blackjack in his barn."

"That makes me feel a little better, I guess. I just hope that his new owner loves him as much as we do."

Heather and her dad stayed with Chauncy until the nurse announced that visiting hours were over. Chauncy had told story after story about famous Morgans and their owners. All of this talk about Morgans and horses in general made Heather realize that she couldn't give up on her dreams. Perhaps one day she would somehow be reunited with Blackjack. Until then, she had to keep working with Rusty and learning everything she could.

Heather continued to work with Rusty almost every day. While Chauncy was at the rehabilitation center, the Richardsons had decided to spend part of every Sunday visiting him. Each visit would start off the same. Chauncy's face would light up when he saw his visitors, and, after the usual small talk that adults always seemed to be obligated to make, he would immediately ask Heather for a progress report on Rusty. He wanted to know everything Heather had been doing with him, not because he really needed to know, but because he just wanted to hear someone talk about horses. From there, the conversation would digress into what had become a favorite topic of Heather's, which was horses of the past. Mr. and Mrs. Richardson would sit quietly and listen, knowing these visits were very important to both Heather and Chauncy.

Meanwhile, Laura continued to stay at her parents' house, taking care of Rusty and running errands for her mother. She occasionally took Rusty out for a short ride, but seemed content to let Heather do most of the riding. After riding every day, Heather would go up to the house to wait for her mom, and it was during these trips to the house that Laura and Heather became good friends. They soon discovered just how much they had in common, from their love of horses to the fact that they had both survived the same horrible English class. Although there was an age difference of a few years, Heather thought of Laura as the big sister she'd never had.

Toward the end of July, Laura mentioned to Heather that there was a three-day horse show that weekend in a neighboring town. "Do you want to go?" she asked.

"I'd love to. What kind of a show is it?"

"It's an open show, which means there will be several different breeds there, all competing against each other. It's a lot of fun. There are usually several Morgans. I know that Mr. MacDonald is normally there—maybe he's bringing Blackjack."

At the mention of Blackjack's name, Heather felt a twinge of excitement and fear. She wanted to see him so badly, just so that she could give him a big hug. But she was also afraid that seeing him would make her miss the horse even more. "I'm sure my parents will let me go. I'll let you know," she said enthusiastically.

Just then, a car horn honked. Heather quickly said her goodbyes to Laura and ran out the door.

Saturday came quickly, and Laura and Heather set off for the horse show. By the time they arrived at the fairgrounds, the show was well under way. Unlike the Morgan event, which had been held at an elaborate facility, this show was at a much smaller location. There was only one little ring, with a few missing boards and very uneven footing. Heather wanted to immediately try and find Mr. MacDonald, but, not wanting to appear rude, she followed Laura to the ring to watch some of the classes instead.

She was fascinated to see so many different types of horses and styles of riding. There were Morgans, Quarter Horses, Arabians, Saddlebreds, Paints, Appaloosas, and Miniature Horses, as well as several other breeds, and all sorts of classes, including saddle seat, western, hunters, jumpers, and driving. All too soon, the activity in the ring concluded as the announcer called for a one-hour lunch break.

"How about some greasy fries?" Laura asked.

"You sound like my dad," Heather laughed. "Sure, I'm pretty hungry."

After a quick lunch, the two friends made their way through the stabling area. Finally, after half an hour of wandering around, Heather saw the dark blue curtains that belonged to Mr. MacDonald and immediately headed for his stalls. Laura, who had been glancing at a beautiful palomino horse, saw Heather walking ahead of her.

"I bet I know where you're going," she teased as she caught up to Heather and tapped her on the shoulder.

Heather looked over at Laura and just smiled. Walking up to Mr. MacDonald's stable area, the girls looked around for Blackjack. They checked all five stalls but, although each stall contained a beautiful Morgan, none of them were Blackjack.

"Looks like they didn't bring him," Laura observed.

"Maybe he's not going very well for them. Maybe he's been acting up," chimed in a somewhat worried Heather. "And now—"

"Well, what a nice surprise!" a man's voice interrupted from behind them.

They turned around to see Mr. MacDonald, along with the same grooms who had been at the Morgan show. Each of them was holding an ice cream cone.

"Hi, Mr. MacDonald!" the girls greeted him in unison.

"How's your dad doing, Laura? I heard he might be home soon."

"Hopefully. You know Dad; he's so cranky that they've been trying to throw him out ever since he got there."

Laura and Mr. MacDonald both laughed. Heather, on the other hand, ignored the comment, anxious to hear news of Blackjack. Mr. MacDonald noticed the concern on Heather's face and asked her, "You're curious about Blackjack, aren't you?"

"Yeah, is he okay?"

"I'm sure he's fine," replied Mr. MacDonald.

The comment, however, increased Heather's anxiety level. "Haven't you seen him?"

"Not for a few weeks," Mr. MacDonald answered. "He was moved to a different trainer's barn in mid-July."

"What happened?" Laura asked.

"Well," Mr. MacDonald said, pausing so that he could choose his words carefully, "he was doing well at my barn. He settled in nicely and had adjusted to the routine. He still had a bit of a problem with his canter, though, and I didn't feel he was ready to show. Mr. Casey, however, didn't agree. He wanted Blackjack shown as soon as possible. Since I wouldn't show him so soon, Mr. Casey decided to move him to a trainer who would."

"Where'd he go?" Laura asked, taking over the difficult position of interrogator for Heather.

"To Jim Spencer," came the answer.

Heather knew she had heard that name before, but she couldn't remember where. She kept saying it over and over again to herself until she remembered. Jim Spencer was the man who was riding the horse who kept running into Blackjack at the Morgan show. The man whom Chauncy had said he wouldn't allow near any of his animals.

"Heather, I'm really, really sorry about this, but there was nothing I could do. Blackjack wasn't my horse. He belongs to Mr. Casey. I couldn't force Mr. Casey to keep the horse with me, nor could I decide where the horse would go. It was all up to him. I'm sure he thought he was doing what was best for the horse, and if things don't work out, he'll move the horse once again."

"Couldn't you have convinced him to keep Blackjack with you?" came the panicky response.

"I tried, Heather, but Mr. Casey was insistent that the horse be shown. I can't show a horse that isn't ready yet. Even though you did a great job with him, Blackjack and I hadn't spent enough time together."

"But if you weren't ready to show him, how could someone else be?" Heather questioned.

"I honestly don't think anyone could get him going in time for the show."

"Is Mr. Spencer here?" Laura asked.

Mr. MacDonald turned to his grooms and asked, "Have you seen him?"

"I thought I saw him at one of the food booths last night," answered the groom who was standing closest to Mr. MacDonald. "Didn't you say you saw him, Jill?"

"Yeah, he had a Saddlebred in a class last night. He had that poor horse so wound up that..." Jill looked over at Heather and realized that it was best not to say any more.

"Do you know where his stalls are?" Heather asked, determined to see Blackjack no matter what it took.

"I think he's over by the entrance to the show grounds," Jill answered.

"Come on, Heather, we might as well go see if we can find Blackjack. Thanks for your help, Mr. MacDonald. I'll tell Dad that we saw you."

"Tell him to hurry up and get back here. I need his help!" Mr. MacDonald chuckled.

"I didn't mean to get upset with you," Heather explained. "I'm just really worried about—"

"You don't need to say any more," Mr. MacDonald said, putting his hands on Heather's shoulders. "I understand what it's like to love a horse so much."

"Thanks," Heather replied as she walked away. Within a few minutes, the two companions had made their way to the stalls where Mr. Spencer was supposed to be.

"Hmmm. I think he must be down here," Laura said, pointing down an aisle in the first barn. "Follow me."

Heather did. Halfway down the aisle, as Heather and Laura walked side by side, a horse came reaching out of its stall, ears flat back, in an attempt to bite Heather.

"Watch it," Laura cautioned as she grabbed Heather and pushed her out of the way. "Not all horses are as nice as ours."

"Hey, what do you think you're doing, bothering my horse?" came a loud, grumpy voice.

There, in front of the two, was a crotchety-looking man, probably in his mid-forties. His brown hair had started to turn gray around the temples, and although he stood up straight, there was a very weathered look to him. He was dressed in a blue polo shirt and tan chinos, and was carrying a riding crop.

Caught off guard, Heather was still able to think quickly. "I'm looking for a horse to buy. I ride saddle seat and had heard that you might have a nice Morgan for sale. By the way, my name is Janet Sanders and this is my sister, Brenda. And you are?"

The man looked at Heather suspiciously while Laura just stood there stone-faced. "I'm Mr. Spencer," he said rudely. "I might have something for sale. It depends on how much you have to spend. You don't look like the sort that could afford my horses."

Heather decided it was time to put her drama training from her Shakespeare class to the test. Her teacher had told her that she had a promising future if she wanted to pursue acting—and now it was time to find out.

"My daddy said I could get whatever horse I wanted," she said coyly. "But he wanted me to get an idea of what was available first. If I see something I like, I'll get him and he'll bring his checkbook."

This was the sort of horrible person who responded best to the mention of money, she thought, and decided to lay it on thick. "My big sister here," she continued as she put her arm around an astounded Laura, "got to get a horse here last year. Daddy paid $20,000 for it. Or was it 25?"

"Huh? Oh, it was only 20," Laura said, trying her best to play along.

"Whatever," sighed Heather. "Do you have anything?"

Baffled by the teenager who seemed to be putting on an act, but unwilling to take a chance at losing out on a possible sale, Mr. Spencer led them to the next stall. Heather looked in and saw a pretty bay mare, with a long flowing mane and tail. But unlike the other Morgans that Heather was used to, this horse did not come over to greet them. Instead, she stayed huddled in the back of the stall as the three people looked in at her.

"Come here, you!" the stern-looking man commanded as he hit the riding crop against the stall door. The horse flinched but didn't come closer. Heather and Laura both jumped slightly.

"Actually, sir, I was looking for something in black. Do you have anything?"

"The only black Morgan I have isn't for sale, and besides, I don't think you could handle him. I've got a nice Saddlebred over here that I think you might like."

"No, I'd rather see the black Morgan," a suddenly pushy Heather demanded. "I have my heart set on a black horse and my daddy just might decide to come up with enough money so that he *will* be for sale."

"He's down here."

Heather and Laura followed the man to the end of the barn, where he pointed to the last stall.

"Don't get too close. He's a mean one."

Then it must not be Blackjack, thought Heather, disappointed that she wouldn't get to see her treasured horse. She approached cautiously and looked in. At the back of the stall stood a black stallion, cowering and trembling.

"Blackjack?" asked the shocked girl, unable to believe what she saw.

The horse turned his head in Heather's direction, but refused to come near her.

"You know this horse?" the heartless man questioned.

"Isn't this the horse that won the Futurity at the Morgan show? It sure looks like him," Heather said, a slight quiver in her voice.

"Yeah it is, but like I said, he's not for sale. If he was, I don't think the owner would part with him for less than $50,000. I doubt that your father would come up with that much now, would he?" he asked, smiling cruelly at the two companions.

"Probably not," Laura admitted, speaking for Heather, who was by now speechless.

"Well, if your father is around and wants to see him go, he's in the fifth class this afternoon. Now if you'll excuse me, I've got work to do. And don't linger in my barn; I don't like to have my horses disturbed by every little kid who comes through here," Mr. Spencer instructed snootily as he walked away.

Heather just stood there, leaning against the stall door, whispering the horse's name over and over. Tears began to fall down her face as the horse stared at her, fear in his eyes. Blackjack was still at the far end of the stall, but slowly, cautiously, he made his way to the front. He stopped just out of Heather's reach, afraid to come close to anybody. Heather could see fresh whip marks on his flanks, what looked like spur marks on his sides, and several small areas where the hair was missing.

"Come on, boy, I won't hurt you," Heather pleaded softly as she held out her hand.

The horse reached out with his nose and sniffed Heather's hand. He took another step so that he was close enough for Heather to pat.

"Oh, Blackjack, I'm so sorry. I'll get you out of here somehow, I promise."

"Didn't I tell you two to get out?" the loud voice of Mr. Spencer suddenly called out.

Blackjack immediately jumped back and clung to the far end of the stall, once again trembling.

"Come on, little sister," Laura gently ordered as she put her arm around Heather and led her out of the barn.

Once they were out of hearing range of Mr. Spencer, Heather burst into tears. "What am I going to do?" she asked through the sobs. "Blackjack has to get out of there. That creep is hurting my horse. I have to get him out of there!"

"Come on, I think we better go home."

"No!" came the response. "I want to ... I mean I *need* to see Blackjack's class. Please, I don't want to go home yet. I need to see Blackjack again."

"It's just going to make it worse, Heather. Come on, let's go home."

"Please, Laura, I don't want to. I'm okay, really," Heather sniffled as she tried unsuccessfully to hold back her tears.

"Okay, but your parents are going to kill me when they find out about this."

The two of them made their way back to the ring, where they found a spot next to the gate. They stood there and watched the first four classes, not saying a word to each other. Heather stared at the ring but didn't see any of the action going on there.

"Hey there, how'd it go?"

Heather and Laura turned around to see Mr. MacDonald.

"Not so good," Laura replied.

"Did you find Blackjack?"

"Yes," sobbed Heather. "And he's terrible. That horrible man has him and he's beating him. You can see the fear in Blackjack's eyes."

"I'm so sorry, Heather," was the only thing Mr. MacDonald could say.

"Why do people do that? How can someone be so mean to a beautiful, innocent animal?"

"I don't know. I only know that, fortunately, there aren't too many people like that."

As they talked, the announcer gave the call for the fifth class, Open English Pleasure. The gate attendant opened the gate as ten horses of various breeds and colors stormed the entrance. Heather looked, but didn't see Blackjack. Confused, she looked at Mr. MacDonald. "Maybe they scratched the class."

Just then, they heard the sound of a whip being cracked, and a familiar, nasty voice hollering, "Get up there! Come on you, get up!"

Blackjack appeared with Mr. Spencer riding, a groom cracking a whip behind them. As they approached the gate, Heather could see that Blackjack had his ears pinned back and was tossing his head from side to side, trying to evade the pressure from the reins, which his rider was holding much too tightly.

"He looks awful," Laura noted as the horse passed them and entered the ring.

As the 11 horses trotted around the ring, Blackjack continued to toss his head and pin his ears. When the announcer called for a walk, the black stallion refused. Instead, he slowly pranced in a nervous sort of gait. When the horses were asked to canter, Blackjack kicked out with his hind legs, barely missing the pretty chestnut mare behind him.

"He's never done that before!" Heather exclaimed. "He's terrified!"

For his actions, Blackjack received a quick slap from Mr. Spencer's crop. The horse responded by kicking again. Then he started to canter, but continued to toss his head. The horses cantered around the ring several times until they were told to walk and reverse. Blackjack once again pranced.

"He's not going to canter this time," Heather warned the others as the class continued. "I know he's not going to."

Heather's prediction turned out to be correct. When the announcer asked for the canter, Blackjack exploded. He backed up, much like he had done when Heather rode him, except that this time he backed up more quickly, moving at an angle so that his hind end was headed for the railing. When he hit the rail, the horse, surprised and confused, had to stop. Since there was now no other way to escape, he reared up. Mr. Spencer almost fell off, but managed to stay on by grabbing Blackjack's mane. When the horse hit the ground, his rider struck him on the flank with the crop. Panic-stricken, the horse reared again, this time also spinning around so that he was facing the wrong way. The other horses, who had already started to canter, reacted by jumping sideways as they approached the frightened horse.

"Number 18 is excused from the ring" came the command from the announcer.

The gate attendant opened the gate and the groom who had been assisting Mr. Spencer dropped her whip and ran into the ring. By the time the groom reached the frightened horse, Mr. Spencer had managed to get him to stop rearing and stand still. The groom grabbed the reins and led the horse out of the ring. Blackjack didn't notice his young friend as he was led passed her, too concerned about his trainer to look around him. But as they passed, Heather noticed that the sweat-drenched horse was trembling. He stopped just a few short steps beyond Heather, and she started to walk toward the horse, hoping that she would be allowed to help him.

"Don't," Laura advised, grabbing Heather's arm. "It will only make it worse."

Heather looked at Laura, not saying a word.

"She's right," Mr. MacDonald agreed. "I've seen that man after a bad class and he can be pretty mean. If he knows you're watching him it will only make him worse, and he'll take it out on the horse."

So Heather just stood there, watching as Mr. Spencer dismounted, put the stirrups up, loosened the girth, and led the horse away. He seemed to have calmed down, and hopefully would not take his anger out on Blackjack.

"Heather, I'll call Mr. Casey tonight. I'll explain what I saw and ask him to consider moving Blackjack."

"Don't you think he's here? Don't you think he wanted to see his horse?"

"Actually, no. Mr. Casey is an investor. He bought the horse as an investment, hoping to make some money. I'd be very surprised if he were here today. Come on, let's get out of here. It's hot and I'm hungry. I'll buy everyone an ice cream."

MAKING A PLAN

On the way home from the show, Heather and Laura talked about what they could do to try to rescue Blackjack. Heather was able to come up with all sorts of suggestions on what should be done to Mr. Spencer, but none of them were terribly realistic. Since robbing a bank to come up with the money to buy Blackjack was slightly illegal, as was stealing him, they were unable to find any real solutions. Admitting defeat for the moment, they agreed to wait and see if Mr. MacDonald had any success with Mr. Casey. Meanwhile, they came to the conclusion that it would be best not to tell Chauncy what had happened, since it would only upset him.

By the time they arrived at Heather's house, Heather had managed to pull herself together. Gone were the tears, replaced by a staunch determination that she would somehow get Blackjack back.

"You're home early," Mrs. Richardson greeted them as the two friends walked into the house. "I didn't expect you until dinner time."

"We left a little early, Mom," Heather began. "Something kinda unexpected happened."

She proceeded to explain the whole story to her mother, telling her about how Blackjack was now with Mr. Spencer, how frightened her horse was, and how terribly he did at the show.

"You should have seen it, Mom, it was awful. Blackjack has been turned into a frightened horse. When Mr. Spencer showed him to me, he didn't recognize me at first. But then after that creep left us alone, Blackjack settled down and started to come over to me, until that jerk came back. Then Blackjack tried to hide at the back of his stall."

"Mr. MacDonald is going to call Mr. Casey to see if he can talk him into moving his horse to another trainer. Maybe that'll work," Laura said hopefully.

"Mom? You can have my allowance for the rest of my life. I'll do anything to rescue Blackjack."

She led Blackjack down the aisle toward the sliding doors and tried to open them, but just like the first time when she was trying to get in, they moved an inch or so and then stopped. She looked down and saw a lock on the floor that was keeping the door from opening. Without thinking, she bent down and unlatched it. As soon as she did this, a loud, blaring alarm went off. "Oh no, we're caught! It's the alarm, the alarm, the alarm!"

Knowing that she would soon be caught, she decided to open the sliding doors and make a run for it. But as she pushed one of the heavy doors to the side, her horse panicked and began to back up. Turning to face him, she pleaded with him to follow her out of the barn.

"Come on, we've got to get out of here, now!" But it was no use; the horse continued to slowly back up, away from the doors. Because her back was facing the sliding doors, she didn't see the man who was running toward them.

"I knew it was you!" came a loud, malicious voice.

The girl spun around. Standing in front of her was a crotchety-looking man, probably in his mid-forties. His brown hair had started to turn gray around the temples, and although he stood up straight, there was a very weathered look to him. He was dressed in a blue polo shirt and tan chinos, and was carrying a riding crop.

Heather jumped out of bed. Her heart was racing and she was sweating slightly. Her dream had once again returned, but this time she could see the face of the evil trainer. It was Mr. Spencer!

On Monday, Heather took Rusty for a quiet trail ride early in the morning. A heat wave had hit and the temperature for the day was expected to reach 95 degrees, with high humidity. To avoid the heat, Heather had convinced her mom to take her to the farm at 8 a.m. By 11 a.m., she had finished riding Rusty, cleaned his stall, and made her way to the house—just as the worst of the day's heat and humidity hit.

"Did you hear from him?" she asked as she entered the house and saw Laura.

Laura, who had been watching television in the living room, turned off the set and replied, "Mr. MacDonald? No. But I don't expect to hear from him for a few days. He's probably got a few other things to take care of after being away at a show. Once things settle down he'll call Mr. Casey. I promise I'll call you as soon as I hear anything."

"Thanks."

That night, while Heather was eating dinner with her mom, the phone rang.

Heather jumped up from her chair and grabbed the phone. "Hello?"

"Heather? It's me, Laura."

"Did he call?"

"Yeah, I just got off the phone with him."

"What did he say?"

"Well, there's good news and bad news. Which do you want to hear first?"

"You better give me the bad news first."

"Okay, well, Mr. Casey said that he was really unhappy with how Blackjack performed but he blamed it all on the horse, not Mr. Spencer."

"How could he do that? Mr. Spencer is such a jerk, anyone could see that—"

"I know that, and you know that, but Mr. Casey doesn't. He isn't a horse person."

"So now what, Laura?"

"Mr. MacDonald told me that Mr. Casey is planning on having Blackjack shown a couple more times."

"That makes a lot of sense," replied Heather very sarcastically.

"I know, pretty stupid, huh? The horse is only going to get worse. Anyway, that's what Mr. MacDonald said, and that's where the good news comes in."

"How could there be any good news?"

"Apparently, Mr. Casey had the same sort of thing happen last year with another horse. He bought the horse in the spring, paid a lot of money for it and then sent it to Mr. Spencer. Evidently the horse had done a lot of winning before Mr. Casey bought it, but like Blackjack, once Mr. Spencer got his hands on the animal, his performances deteriorated to the point where they could no longer show the horse. They wound up selling the horse in the Fall Consignment Sale for next to nothing. Someone bought it real cheap, got the horse to a good trainer, and over the winter they were able to bring the horse back. Now he's winning again."

"Mr. MacDonald told you all that?"

"Yeah. He didn't want to get your hopes up, but he thinks the same thing may happen to Blackjack."

"When is that Fall Sale?"

"I think it's the second Saturday in September. I can check it out for you. But I believe what we really need to do right now is wait and see how Blackjack does at the next couple of shows. It sounds kinda weird, but I guess we should hope that he does pretty bad."

"What a bizarre thought, but yeah, you're right."

"I'll keep my fingers crossed."

"Thanks, Laura, but do you really think if I got him back, I could bring him around?"

"Heather, if anyone can, you can. Remember, he came over to you. He was afraid, but he still came over to you. That's because he trusts you and that's what you need to bring him around: trust."

"I hope you're right."

"I am."

"Okay," Heather paused, thinking. "I'll see you tomorrow. Bye."

"Bye."

And she hung up the phone.

The following day, after she had worked Rusty, Heather made her usual trip up to the Campbell's house to wait for her mom. When she rang the bell, she was surprised to hear a voice that she'd not heard for a while.

"Come on in, young lady."

"Chauncy?" Heather squealed as she opened the screen door. "You're home! Why didn't anyone tell me you were coming home?"

Chauncy was sitting in his favorite recliner, reading a book. "Because nobody told me until yesterday."

"Actually, they threw him out," a voice hollered from the kitchen. In walked Mrs. Campbell, followed by Laura.

"Dad was driving them all nuts. The nurses were threatening to go on strike if he didn't leave," Laura teased.

"I wasn't that bad," Chauncy said, trying to defend himself.

"I heard one of the nurses complain that all the horse talk was making her crazy," Heather joked, getting in on the fun.

"Hey come on! Isn't anyone going to defend me?" Chauncy pleaded.

"Nope," Laura said.

"Not me," Heather agreed.

"Don't expect *me* to come to your defense!" Mrs. Campbell laughed as she walked over to Chauncy and gave him a big hug and kiss. "But I still love you!"

"When did you get home?"

"Yesterday afternoon."

"Have you been down to the barn yet?"

"Yup, as soon as I got home. Rusty looks great, Heather. You did a wonderful job with him this summer."

"Thanks, Chauncy."

"How about Blackjack? Any news?"

Heather and Laura looked at each other. Heather didn't know what to say.

"Uhh, we, uhh," Laura said, stumbling over her words. "We haven't, umm, haven't heard anything. I assume he's doing fine. Maybe we'll see him at one of the shows this fall."

"Oh," Chauncy replied. "That's strange. I thought Tom would have dropped us a note or something. I'll have to give him a call when I get a chance."

"So when are you going to take Rusty for a drive?" Heather asked in an attempt to change the subject.

"Probably not for a little while," Mrs. Campbell replied, speaking for her husband. "I know that Chauncy would love to get out there today and go for a drive, but I've got strict orders from his doctor for him to take it easy for a little while."

"That means she'll never let me go for a drive with Rusty," Chauncy moaned, rolling his eyes.

"No, that means you've got to take it easy for a week or so."

"Yes dear, whatever you say dear," Chauncy retorted in a teasing voice.

The rest of the summer went by quickly. Heather continued to ride Rusty every day and Chauncy did start driving his horse soon after returning home. Mrs. Campbell, however, watched him like a mother hen and kept his horse activities to a minimum. Heather and Laura managed to keep their secret about Blackjack simply by never talking about him in front of Chauncy, and by changing the subject whenever Chauncy mentioned his name. But they knew that Chauncy would eventually find out what had happened. Still, whenever Chauncy was not around, Heather and Laura frequently talked about Blackjack and how he might be doing. Heather had also hoped for some more news about the horse, but Mr. MacDonald never called back.

Finally, during the last week of August, news of Blackjack came. Heather had just finished riding Rusty and was brushing the horse's face while he stood quietly on the cross ties.

"Hey, Heather!" Laura whispered as she entered the barn. "I just got some news that I thought you

189

might want to hear. But I wanted to make sure Dad wasn't here."

"No, he's not here. I think he went out with your mom for a little while."

"Oh yeah, I forgot."

"You can stop whispering now."

"Sorry."

"You can stop apologizing, too."

"Will you cut that out!" Laura ordered, who was by now used to Heather's teasing.

"Okay," Heather laughed. "I'll stop. So what's your news?"

"It's about Blackjack."

"What?" Heather asked, raising her voice slightly. "What did you hear?"

"My friend Karen called last night. She lives near Mr. Spencer. Last time we talked back in July I told her what was going on and she promised to call if she heard anything. Well, last week she was at a local show and saw Blackjack. Mr. Spencer was leading the horse around behind the stable area before the show started and she said Blackjack looked terrible. She's not sure what happened after that since he got scratched from every class he was supposed to go in. But the next day she met someone who had seen Blackjack at another show and they told Karen the horse was dangerous. He struck at another horse in the ring and got excused.

There's even a rumor that he tried to attack Mr. Spencer."

"Oh my gosh," Heather said, dropping the brush.

"I don't think they're going to try to show him anymore. In fact, I bet Mr. Casey is putting him in that Fall Consignment Sale that I told you about. I called Mr. MacDonald, but he didn't know whether or not Blackjack had been consigned. He said he had a copy of the catalog and Blackjack wasn't listed. But a lot of times horses get added at the last minute and don't make it into the catalog."

"Are you going?"

"I'd like to. You know that I'm leaving for school this weekend, but I think I'll be able to come back for the auction."

"How are we going to do this? I mean, I still have the $300 in my savings account and could probably get Dad to agree to loan me the $700 that he was going to give me last time. But I don't think that'll be enough. What about trailering, and boarding and—"

"Heather, I think you're getting ahead of yourself. Don't worry about all that other stuff. Just keep your fingers crossed that Blackjack is actually in the sale and that nobody else wants him. Besides, I can always bring Dad's trailer. I'll just tell him that we're going to the auction to look for a horse for you. I'm sure Dad won't mind if you keep him here. Actually, he'd love it."

"What are you two ladies talking about?"

191

Heather and Laura turned toward the sound of the voice, and there was Chauncy leaning against the barn door.

"Nothing," Heather replied.

"Just talking about Rusty. How long have you been standing there, Dad?"

"Just got here. Your mother and I had to go into town to buy some snacks so she could put together a 'care package' for you. You know your mother, she'd never send you back to college without plenty of food for your dorm."

"Of course she gives me enough food to feed the whole school!" Laura laughed.

"I tried to get her to buy less, but I'm afraid I wasn't very successful. I think she bought even more food this time."

"Oh, no, just what I need," Laura groaned.

The first week of September rolled around all too soon. Although Heather missed Blackjack terribly and worried about him on a daily basis, she also enjoyed her time with Rusty. Her dad had been right; Rusty had helped her get through the strain of worrying constantly about the black stallion. He was a kind, gentle horse who would put up with almost anything and was always willing to lend an ear. But now all those long, relaxing days with Rusty were to be replaced with the rigors of school.

School, fortunately, did not mean an end to riding, as Heather was able to ride Rusty every day. She started taking a different bus after school, one that had a stop right near Chauncy's house, and would ride Rusty for an hour or so until her mom came to pick her up.

Heather had told her parents about the upcoming sale. Her dad agreed to once again loan her $700, but since he was going to be away on business the week of the sale, he arranged to have a check ready before he left. He gave Heather strict orders not to let the check out of her sight and to rip it up into tiny little pieces if she was unable to buy Blackjack.

Laura picked Heather up at 7 a.m. that Saturday.

It was a cool and rainy day, too early in the fall for such dismal weather. Despite that, Heather was in a pretty good mood, if a little bit nervous. She had a good feeling about today.

The two friends had a lot of catching up to do since they hadn't seen each other in over two weeks, when Laura had left for college. Laura told Heather all about her new classes, what life was like in the dorms, and what she did for fun while at school. Heather then told her friend all about her new classes. Eventually the conversation drifted to the topic of horses. Heather talked about all she and Rusty had done in the past two weeks, and then finally asked, "So what do you think our chances are?"

"Chances for what?"

193

"For buying Blackjack!"

"Geeze, I don't know. I don't want to get your hopes up, but then again I can't see him going for a lot of money, not after what I've heard about him lately. Let's just keep our fingers crossed."

By the time they arrived at the sale, the rain had become heavy and the windshield wipers were working furiously to keep the window clear.

"Great, this is all we need," sighed Laura. "The last thing I want to do today is get stuck in the mud! I can see myself trying to explain *that* one to Dad."

Once parked, they made a mad dash for the arena and managed to get there without getting too wet. After shaking the rain out of her hair, Heather took a quick look around. There were lots of people wandering around, talking and eating donuts or drinking soda. She couldn't see any horses, although there were about ten rows of chairs set up near the front facing a podium, most of which were already filled. There was an aisle going down the center so that people could easily get to their chairs. This aisle, however, was currently crowded with large groups of people who were busy talking among themselves.

"What now?" she asked.

"The sale should be starting soon, so let's just find a good place to stand and..." Laura paused as she reached over to a table and grabbed a booklet. "Let's get one of these and look for Blackjack."

Heather followed suit and picked up a sales catalog. The two friends thumbed through the sale listings, but were disappointed to see that Blackjack wasn't listed.

"Oh hey," Laura exclaimed. "There's Mr. MacDonald! Mr. MacDonald? Hi, how ya doing?"

Mr. MacDonald, who had been talking to a small group of people a short distance away, waved. Then he turned his attention back to those to whom he had been talking.

"Oh well, he's probably working on some business deal. Come on, let's go," Laura suggested.

The auction started shortly thereafter, with the auctioneer, a stout man clad in blue jeans and a short-sleeved white cotton shirt, making a brief announcement about the high quality of the animals in the sale.

"More likely the castoffs no one wants to feed over the winter," sneered a young man standing next to Heather. He was trying to impress his partner, a pretty woman with long blonde hair, probably about twenty, who was dressed in very tight designer jeans and a frilly, light tan blouse. She was doing her best to ignore her companion. Heather glanced at the man, more in disgust than in curiosity. He was probably about the same age as the woman but unlike her, he was dressed in torn and dirty jeans and a once-white shirt that looked like it could use a good washing.

A moment later, the first horse entered the arena: a gray Arabian mare. A little girl who was smiling from ear to ear rode her. The horse trotted boldly toward the podium and passed it without flinching. As the mare reached the side of the arena, the rider slowed her down to a walk. Then the small girl carefully turned her horse so they could trot past the podium again. Back and forth they went as the auctioneer began his sales pitch.

"Our first lot is a wonderful Arabian mare who has proven to be a great, bombproof horse. Just look at the smile on her rider's face. This horse is a very young-looking 25 years old and—"

"Has one foot in the grave already," laughed the annoying young man.

Heather shot him a vicious glance.

"Hey, Laura," whispered Heather. "Can we go look at the horses in the barns to see if Blackjack is here?"

"No, I think we should stay put. He could be almost anywhere and we may never find him. Besides, sometimes they stick the unlisted horses in between the ones who are in the catalog. We don't want to miss him, so let's not go wandering off."

The sale continued for another hour and a half. The auctioneer had several assistants, who, like the assistants at Chauncy's auction, helped get bids from the audience. Once the bidding had stopped, the auctioneer would continue to try to get bids for another five minutes or so. Eventually, he would realize nobody was going to bid any more, holler "Sold!" and then ask for the next lot.

As for the horses who were going through the sale, they were a sorry lot. Heather didn't want to admit that the obnoxious man standing next to her was right, but he probably was. There were several very old horses, numerous ones who seemed to be lame, and many that gave their riders trouble. One of the horses was so terrified that he refused to go anywhere near the podium.

"That look, see that look?" Heather asked Laura.

"Yeah?"

"It's the same look that Blackjack had."

"Probably trained by Jim Spencer," sighed Laura. Most of the horses didn't sell for very much money, although the few that didn't seem to have any obvious problems sold for a good price.

"Those are the ones you've got to be careful about," Laura warned. "At least with the lame horses you know what's wrong with them, but with the ones which look okay there's frequently something else wrong that you can't see. Most people who have a good horse are not going to sell it here."

Heather's attention had turned to Mr. MacDonald. The sale had become pretty depressing, with so many once wonderful horses being sold off to uncertain futures. Mr. MacDonald was still talking to the group of people they had seen him with earlier, largely ignoring the sale. Heather couldn't figure out why he had come if he wasn't bidding.

"Hey! Look!" Laura exclaimed as she gently hit Heather on the arm to get her attention.

Heather turned her attention to the side entrance where all of the sale horses had entered. What she saw made her heart race. A black Morgan, soaking wet from the rain, trotted into the arena. He had a leather show bridle on with a gold and red patent leather browband. His head hung low, his tail was clamped tightly to his body, and his eyes were half closed. Leading the horse was Jim Spencer.

"Oh my gosh, it's Blackjack!" Heather exclaimed.

"Hey, look at that one," said the young man next to Heather. "I've heard about him. He's a nut case. Tried to attack his trainer for no reason. A real dangerous horse. If you ask me they should sell him for glue!"

"No one is asking you, you jerk!" Heather said angrily as she grabbed Laura by the arm and walked away. They were able to get a good spot right behind the last row of chairs. A spot where one of the assistants was sure to see them when they bid.

Mr. Spencer led the once proud horse up toward the podium. The horse looked like all he wanted to do was lay down.

"What's wrong with him?" Heather asked.

"Looks like they drugged him. Probably the only way they could get him here," Laura explained. Seeing the worried look on Heather's face, she continued, "Don't worry. It'll wear off."

"Our next lot is a marvelous Morgan stallion," the auctioneer interrupted. "His registered name is Gallant Image, although I'm told his barn name is Dudley."

Heather and Laura just looked at each other, unable to figure out how anyone could come up with such a name.

"He has great breeding, has won several major Morgan awards, and is sure to continue winning for you. Now, who'll start the bidding at $500?"

Heather's hand shot up before the auctioneer had even finished his sentence. But one of the assistants who was working the front row announced, "Here, we have it here!"

Heather, upset and alarmed that her bid went unnoticed, quickly walked to the front. Her hand was raised before the announcer even asked for another bid.

"You bid $1000?" he asked Heather. She nodded her head yes.

"Do I hear $1200?"

"Yes!" hollered one of the assistants.

"$1500?" asked the auctioneer as he looked at Heather.

Again she nodded her head 'yes.'

"Hey, what do you think you're doing?" whispered Laura, who had quietly walked up behind her. "You don't have that kind of money."

"I know, but I can't lose him now. I'll get the money somehow," she explained. She was sure that Blackjack would soon be hers.

"$1600!" yelled a voice from the back.

Heather and Laura turned to see someone new enter the bidding. Before they knew it, the bidder in the front row increased his bid to $2000. Heather knew that, although she probably could have convinced her dad to loan her a little more money, there was no way he would give her over $2000. As the bidding continued, she began to realize that she had lost her beloved horse again.

"What about $2200?" asked the auctioneer as he looked at Heather.

She slowly shook her head 'no.'

"I have it back here," shouted one of the assistants.

"And $2300?" asked the auctioneer, looking toward the front row. The bidder, whom Heather could not see, apparently agreed with the price since the auctioneer next asked for $2500.

"I've got it!" announced the assistant from the back.

Once $2500 was reached, however, no one wanted to bid further. The auctioneer, in his usual fashion, kept asking for a higher bid for several more minutes. Finally, as his gavel was about to go down, someone from far back in the audience hollered, "$2600!"

Everyone turned to see who had bid. Heather was surprised to see that it was Mr. MacDonald. But unlike the last auction, Heather was not relieved. She knew that the stallion had ended up going to an uncaring owner the first time and she feared that it was about to happen all over again.

"That's $2600! I have $2600. Do I hear $2700?" The auctioneer, now encouraged to continue his sales pitch, threw in a comment about what a gorgeous animal Blackjack was. But there were no additional bids and so finally he announced, "Sold!" as his gavel fell.

Heather just stood there, too stunned to move. She stared at Mr. MacDonald, who seemed to be looking right at her.

"I'm so sorry," Laura consoled her. "Come on, let's get out of here."

Heather turned to see Blackjack being led away. She couldn't believe that she had lost him again. As Laura took Heather's arm to guide her out of the building, Mr. MacDonald began to walk over to them.

"I don't want to talk to him, Laura."

"Too late for that!" Mr. MacDonald replied.

"What do you want?" asked Heather coldly.

"Hey, is that any way to talk to the guy who just bought a horse for you?"

"What are you talking about?" Heather asked.

"Well I know you're upset, but you really shouldn't be. Especially since you're now a horse owner."

"Would you please tell me what the heck you're talking about?" Heather insisted.

"I didn't want to tell you earlier, but I got a call from your dad a few days ago. He had been thinking about the sale and was worried that you might not have enough money to buy your horse. Since he's been out of town, there was nothing that he could do himself so he asked me to take care of it. He gave me a dollar limit and told me to bid up to that amount. But he really wanted you to buy the horse so he asked me not to get involved unless the bidding went over the $1000 that you had."

Heather looked at him, perplexed.

"Don't you get it?" Laura asked. "Your dad just bought Blackjack for you!"

Heather looked at Laura, then back at Mr. MacDonald. She couldn't believe what she was hearing, and it took a minute to sink in. She turned back to Laura who had a huge smile on her face, and then at Mr. MacDonald, who was now grinning from ear to ear.

She screamed so loudly that everyone in the arena turned to look at her. "I love you! I love you!" she hollered as she reached over and hugged Mr. MacDonald. "Thank you! Thank you! Thank you!" she shrieked as she ran out the door to find her horse.

GAINING TRUST

The rain had slowed down to a slight drizzle when
Heather rushed out of the arena and began her
search for Blackjack. The horse had been led away a
few minutes before she had received the good news,
and now was nowhere to be seen. Anxious to find
him, she asked the first person she saw. "Did anyone
see a black Morgan come through here?"

"Gotta be more specific, kid. There have been
lots of horses going by here today," replied a crusty
old man dressed in denim work clothes.

"I'm looking for um, er, a black Morgan stallion,"
Heather answered, stumbling over her words. "He
was just sold a few minutes ago, and was being led
by a man named Jim Spencer."

"Nah," the old man replied gruffly. "Don't know
anyone by that name."

"Sure you do, Dad," interrupted a man in his
mid-thirties, a young replica of the older man. "You
know Jim, good ol' Jim. Remember the party last
year?"

"Oh yeah," the elderly man said slowly. "He's the one who had all those great horse stories, right? Didn't he just go by here?"

By now Heather was getting annoyed. "Please, if you've seen him, would you mind telling me which way he went?"

"I think he went that way," the old man offered, pointing to the next barn.

"No he didn't, Dad. He went into the barn over there," the young man corrected, pointing to a barn further away.

"Thank you," Heather replied as she ran off.

By the time she reached the barn, she was out of breath. She entered the building, looked down the long, dark aisle at the forty or so stalls, and began her search. There were stalls on both sides of the aisle and she went from side to side looking into each, careful not to miss one. Most of the stalls were empty, with the exception of just a few, which had horses silently eating hay in them. Finally, she came to the last stall on the right side of the aisle. The door was open, and when Heather looked in she saw a man facing away from her, a horse standing quietly behind him. Because it was a gray, dismal day, it was hard to see into the stall.

"Excuse me, I'm looking for a horse—"

The man turned around and Heather immediately realized that it was Mr. Spencer. Caught off guard, she didn't know what to say. Mr. Spencer walked toward her and, as he got closer, smiled a crooked smile. "I know you," he said cruelly. "You're the girl who tried to buy one of my horses. The one who had a rich daddy."

"I don't know what you're talking about," Heather replied, not wanting to admit to the past charade.

"Yeah, that was you," he continued as he walked out of the stall. Heather backed up a few steps until she was against the wall. "Your name is Janet and your sister was Brenda or Barrie or something like that. Or was that all an act?"

"Look, I don't know what you're talking about. I'm just looking for Gallant Image. I just bought him and I'd like to—"

"Yeah, you're the one. Well, it doesn't really matter now, does it? You bought this horse, huh? You think you're just going to ride off into the sunset with him, don't you? Ha! Boy, are you in for a big surprise, kid! This horse is crazy. I'm glad to be rid of him."

"Can I just see my horse, please?"

"How do I know you're the one who bought him? Can't take any chances now, can I? Might get sued if you get hurt. So why don't you just go on home now, little girl?"

Heather was starting to become frightened. Mr. Spencer seemed very upset and she didn't know what to do. She was too afraid to walk past him into the stall, but was also reluctant to leave her horse in the hands of this horrible man.

"Come on, kid. What are you waiting for? Get out of here!"

"I think she'd like to see her horse," came a man's voice from down the aisle.

Heather and Mr. Spencer both turned to see Mr. MacDonald and Laura walking toward them. Heather felt an enormous sense of relief when she saw the two of them.

"I've got the paperwork right here," Mr. MacDonald continued as he pulled some papers from his pocket. "This should be all you need. Everything has been taken care of."

"Let me see that," Mr. Spencer demanded.

Mr. Spencer mumbled to himself as he looked over the papers. "Looks all right. Yeah, I guess he's all yours. Good luck!" He snickered as he passed the papers back to Mr. MacDonald and walked away.

"Heather, are you okay?" Laura asked.

"Yeah, he just scared me a little."

Turning her attention to the open stall, Heather cautiously walked in.

"Careful," Mr. MacDonald warned.

Blackjack was standing in the far corner of the stall, head hanging low.

"Blackjack?" Heather whispered. "I'm back. You're safe now."

The horse didn't even look up at her.

"What's wrong with him?" she asked, to no one in particular.

Mr. MacDonald and Laura walked into the stall. "Look at his eyes," Mr. MacDonald said. "See how they're glazed over? He's been drugged."

"Will it hurt him?"

"No, but I would suggest that you girls get him in the trailer as soon as possible and get him home. Once that stuff wears off, he may be rather difficult to deal with."

"I think that's a good idea," Laura agreed. Heather stood quietly next to her horse, gently stroking his neck. It felt so good to be close to him again, even if he was ignoring her.

"Here, Heather, put this lead rope on," Laura said, handing Heather a cotton lead rope.

Heather took the lead and attached it to Blackjack's halter, an old, cracked leather contraption that was partially held together with bailing twine.

"Heather, why don't you let me take him? He's apt to be a bit wobbly right now. I don't want him falling on you," Mr. MacDonald offered.

Mr. MacDonald took the horse and carefully led him away. Heather and Laura quietly followed, not saying a word. Once at the trailer, the horse walked right on, seemingly unaware of where he was. Mr. MacDonald tied Blackjack to the cross ties while Laura and Heather closed up the back of the trailer.

"Okay, girls, you better get going," Mr. MacDonald advised them.

"Thank you so much," Heather said. She walked over to Mr. MacDonald and gave him a big hug. "You have no idea how much this means to me!"

"I think I do," he said, smiling.

The girls got into the truck and as soon as Laura started driving, Heather asked, "Did you know what was going on?"

"What?"

"What my dad and Mr. MacDonald were up to? You did make a point of saying hi to Mr. MacDonald."

"No, honestly," chuckled Laura. "I didn't have a clue."

"Really?"

"You think I could have kept it secret from you?"

"No, I guess you're right."

"I'm just glad that it all worked out so well."

"Thanks, Laura. You've been a good friend and I owe you."

About ten minutes from the farm, Blackjack started kicking the trailer.

"What's he doing?" Heather asked, concerned that her horse might get injured.

"I think the tranquilizer is wearing off. It's a good thing we're almost home!"

As they got closer to Chauncy's, the kicking got more frequent ... and louder.

"I hope he doesn't get hurt," Heather mumbled.

"I hope he doesn't hurt the trailer!" Laura said.

Finally they pulled into the yard. As they got out of the truck the kicking continued, and the horse began to whinny too.

"What on earth do you have in there?" Chauncy asked as he walked up to the trailer.

"Uh oh," Heather whispered in a rather nervous voice.

"Hi, Dad. You'll never guess what—"Laura began meekly.

"Well, let me try. Blackjack wound up with Jim Spencer, who of course, really messed him up. As he usually does, Mr. Spencer put the horse in the Fall Consignment Sale and you two just had to go off and buy him. How's that?"

Heather and Laura looked at each other, dumbfounded.

"How'd you know?" Heather asked, unable to figure out how Chauncy had discovered their plans.

"You've got to give me some credit. Just because I've been sick doesn't mean that I'm totally out of touch. I called Tom shortly after I got home and found out about everything. I didn't want to step in because I know that Blackjack and Heather have a very special bond. Because of that relationship, I think the horse really should belong to Heather and I knew that you," he said as he looked right in Heather's eyes, "were determined to get him back. If anyone could, it was you."

"I think you're right," Laura agreed.

"Now, as for you and your horse, young lady," Chauncy continued, "you can keep him here as long as you muck both stalls, feed both him and Rusty when my wife and I decide to visit our grandchildren, and let me have his first foal!"

"It's a deal!" Heather agreed happily.

At just that instant, Blackjack kicked the trailer so hard that it rocked slightly.

"Now, I think we better get that horse out of there!" Chauncy suggested. "His stall is all ready. I just put fresh bedding in there."

"You knew? You knew that we were able to buy him? How?" his daughter asked.

"Tom called me about an hour ago. I think he was still at the sale."

Blackjack kicked the trailer again.

"Come on. I'll lead him out after you two get the ramp down. But be careful," he cautioned as he walked over to the side door. He opened the door, walked in, and said, "Well hello there, old man. It's good to have you back."

Heather and Laura walked over to the back of the trailer and carefully lowered the ramp. Blackjack immediately tried to back up, but the strap that was behind his rump was still attached.

"Ramp down?" Chauncy hollered.

"Yes," both girls answered in unison.

"Okay, I've got him. Undo the butt strap," he instructed.

"Be careful, Heather. Don't get behind him," Laura warned.

Heather walked up the ramp to the side of Blackjack, being careful not to get too close to his back legs. Staying as far away as possible, she reached over and undid the strap. "Okay," she said.

"Let's go, boy," Chauncy ordered gently.

Heather and Laura quickly got out of the way as Chauncy led the horse out of the trailer. As soon as he was off the ramp, Blackjack's head shot up and he gave an ear-deafening whinny. Then he reached out with his right front leg and struck at his handler. Chauncy instantly snapped the lead and said, "Here now, we'll have none of that." In retaliation, the horse reared up and struck out again.

Chauncy again snapped the lead and was able to get the horse under control. Heather suddenly had a sinking feeling. What had she done? How could she buy a horse who was dangerous? Maybe Mr. Spencer was right and there was no way that she was ever going to get her gentle, loving horse back.

"Looks like we're going to have our hands full," Chauncy said as he led the horse into the barn. Heather and Laura followed at a safe distance from the horse.

Once in his stall, Blackjack focused his attention on the several flakes of hay that Chauncy had put in there.

"That will keep him busy for a while," Chauncy commented. Seeing Heather's concerned expression, he continued, "He's just frightened right now, and doesn't know what to do. Since he's gotten used to being hurt, he thinks that he has to protect himself. But he'll settle down. Don't worry. It may take a while, but we'll get him to relax."

Chauncy shut the stall door and put the lead on the halter hook. Laura and Heather cautiously walked over and peered into the stall.

"Dad, shouldn't we take that awful halter off him?"

"Not till he settles down a bit, Laura. I don't want to struggle to get hold of him."

Heather hung her head down low, resting it on her arms, which were draped over the stall door. "Did I just make a huge mistake, Chauncy?"

Chauncy paused before answering her, as if he was trying to find just the right words. "No, I don't think you did. Blackjack has had a bad experience. He'll always remember it and will probably be less trusting of people because of it. But he also remembers you, and the trust that he had in you. You've got to work with that trust and bring him back. Here, come with me."

In retaliation, the horse reared up and struck out again.

Chauncy walked up to the front of the barn and entered the tack room. He opened the top of the grain bin and handed Heather a scoop of grain.

"The best way to reach a horse is through his stomach. Try feeding this to him."

Heather took the scoop and returned to the stall. "Should I go in?" she asked.

"Not yet. Try giving him a small handful over the door. Let's see what he does."

Heather took a small handful of grain and handed the scoop to Laura. "Here, boy, come here."

Blackjack ignored her and continued to eat his hay.

"Come on Blackjack, look what I've got for you," she continued.

But still the horse ignored her.

"Laura, tap the scoop on the wall. He'll know what that means," Chauncy suggested.

Laura did as told, and the horse's head immediately shot up.

"That's right, boy, come here!"

Blackjack looked at Heather and slowly came over to her. He stopped just out of reach.

"Here it is, Blackjack. Your favorite—grain! That's it, sniff it."

Blackjack stretched his neck out as far as he could, trying to get the grain without having to come too close. His muzzle just barely touched Heather's hand, and as he moved it, several pieces of grain fell to the ground. The horse took a step forward.

"Now move your hand back a little."

Heather did as she was told. Blackjack took another step forward. He was now able to comfortably reach the hand and began to nibble. Heather reached up with her free hand to stroke the horse's neck, but as soon as Blackjack saw the second hand he jumped back.

"He's really afraid, isn't he?" she asked.

"Somebody must have really hurt him," Chauncy observed, the irritation in his voice obvious. "Just do the same thing again, Heather. You've got to take it very slowly."

Heather held the handful of grain out again. "Come on, Blackjack. That was good, wasn't it? Do you want some more?"

The horse looked at Heather for a moment and then came toward her. This time he walked right up to her and began to eat the grain. Again Heather reached out with her free hand, and this time Blackjack didn't jump. He flinched slightly as she touched him, but then he relaxed.

"Give me some more grain," Heather whispered to Laura.

Laura took a fistful of grain from the scoop and put it in Heather's hand. The horse continued to eat it while Heather ran her hand along his neck.

"That's not so bad, is it? Kinda feels good. Remember how I used to brush you all the time? You were so spoiled, and you know what? You're going to be spoiled all over again, except this time no one is going to take you away."

As Heather spoke, Blackjack finished eating the grain in her hand and began to look for more.

"You really think you're going to get more?" Heather asked, feeling relieved at how quickly Blackjack was relaxing.

The stallion shook his head up and down.

"You remembered! Oh, Blackjack, I missed you so much," she said as she fed him the rest of the grain.

After the grain was gone, Blackjack asked for more. Finally convinced that he wasn't going to get any, he went back to eating his hay.

"Let's leave him alone," Chauncy suggested. "He needs time to just relax."

That night, when Heather's dad returned from his business trip, he was accosted at the door by a very excited daughter.

"Dad! Dad! We did it, we did it!" Heather yelled as she rushed toward him and gave him the biggest hug possible. "Thank you so much!"

"I take it you're happy with the outcome?" Mr. Richardson said.

"Of course. But when did you decide to talk to Mr. MacDonald? And why didn't you tell me?"

"I called Tom a few days ago. I didn't want him to say anything to you before the sale because I couldn't be sure how much Blackjack would sell for and I could only afford to bid so much. Anyway, I'm glad that it all worked out. So—" He paused to take his tie off. "How'd it go after you got your new horse home?"

Heather told her dad about Blackjack, how he had been tranquilized, his reactions as the drug wore off, and of finally taking some grain from his new owner. He seemed a bit concerned about the horse kicking in the trailer and warned his daughter to be very careful.

The next day when she arrived at the barn, Heather saw her horse contentedly munching on a large pile of hay. Blackjack, upon seeing her, raised his head slightly, nickered, and then went back to his food. She carefully opened the stall door and went in. She was ready to jump out at the first sign of aggression from her horse ... but it didn't happen. He just ignored her.

"Apparently food is more important to you than I am?" she asked him softly. She walked over to him and ran her hand along his back. "You feel so good and I can't believe that I finally have you back. You'll never leave me again, do you hear?"

As the horse continued to eat his hay, Heather silently watched him. Once the hay was gone, Blackjack walked over to his friend and began to rub his head on her chest. "You really do remember, don't you?"

"Of course he does," Chauncy answered as he walked up to the stall.

"Look at how good he's doing, Chauncy! He knows I'd never hurt him."

"You're right. But I think our problem is going to be with riding him."

"I'm not riding him today, am I?" Heather asked, not sure she wanted to attempt riding so soon.

"Nooo," Chauncy said, drawing out the word for effect. "He's not ready for that yet. I think that you two need to become reacquainted first." Heather nodded, and Chauncy continued, "Now, I've got something for you."

"What?" she asked, curious.

Chauncy lifted up his right arm, which he had been hiding behind his back. Heather was thrilled to see the halter that her parents had given her for her birthday. "Where'd you get that?"

"Laura knew that it was important to you, so right before our sale she took it off Blackjack. Now take that horrible piece of junk off your horse's head and put this one on."

Heather reached over and removed the old, broken leather halter from her horse. She handed it to Chauncy and took her halter. As she turned to put it on, Blackjack started rubbing his face on her leg so hard that it almost knocked her over. It was as if he were trying to rub off the feeling and smell of the dilapidated halter.

"Come on, Blackjack. Cut it out. No, don't do that, put your head up so I can get this on."

The horse ignored her and continued to rub. Heather pushed Blackjack's head away from her leg and then gently raised it so that she could slip the halter on.

"Good, now bring him up to the cross ties and give him a good grooming."

Heather led the stallion to the cross ties, snapped the hooks to his halter, grabbed a few brushes from the tack room, and got to work.

"Wellllll," Chauncy said slowly as he ran his hand over Blackjack's back, just behind the withers, "will you look at this?"

"What? What's wrong?" Heather asked.

"See that?" Chauncy said, pointing to a small area of bare skin about the size of a quarter.

"What is it?"

"That, Heather, is called a saddle sore, and it was most definitely one of the reasons why Mr. Spencer had so many problems with Blackjack. Watch this," he said. He put his hand over the sore and applied a little bit of pressure. Blackjack immediately swished his tail, pinned his ears flat back, and flinched his back slightly, as if he were trying to get away from the pain. "See that? It hurt him. And every time Mr. Spencer put his saddle on Blackjack, he was in pain. How on earth could he expect this horse to behave? I'd like to get my hands on that idiot and—"

"Will he be okay?"

"Oh sure he will. See? If you look closely you can see that the hair has already started to grow back. He probably hasn't been ridden since the last show, whenever that was. Hold on, I've got some ointment in the tack room."

Chauncy disappeared into the back of the tack room while Heather and Blackjack just waited. He returned a few moments later with a little green tin. "Just a little dab of this every day for a week or so should do the job," he explained. "As well as a properly fitted saddle once this is healed."

Heather finished grooming the horse and then turned him out in the ring. She was at first reluctant to lead him outside, after seeing what he had done the day before, but Chauncy reassured her and agreed to walk beside them. Blackjack was the perfect gentleman until Heather let him loose in the ring. He immediately squealed out in delight as he reared up and spun around. When he landed, he kicked out with his hind feet and then ran around the ring several times. Heather made her escape as the horse was rearing, and watched the rest of his antics from outside the ring.

The remainder of the day was spent just playing with Blackjack. He stayed out in the ring for over an hour, and then Heather caught him and returned him to his stall. His young owner stayed with him until her mother came to pick her up.

After about a week, Chauncy came into the barn while Heather had her horse on the cross ties and announced, "His back is all healed, so I think you should start riding him."

"Really? I'm not sure that we're ready to—"

"You've got to start sometime. We'll take it slowly, and if you feel that you don't want to go on, you can stop. Okay?"

"All right."

Heather tacked up the horse, grabbed her helmet, and led him out to the ring, where Chauncy was waiting. Chauncy tightened the girth and let the stirrups down. Heather mounted cautiously, expecting Blackjack to act up at any moment. But it didn't happen. As Chauncy stepped away, Heather asked her horse to walk. At first the horse refused. He just stood there, afraid to move. Heather could feel every muscle in his body tense up until he felt like he was about to explode. She clucked to him and lightly tapped him with her heels. Still, Blackjack refused to move.

Chauncy stepped up to them and gently took the reins. He led the horse for a few steps and then let go. "Talk to him, Heather. He's afraid and he needs to know that you're not Jim Spencer."

"Come on, boy, you're okay. Don't worry. I won't hurt you. That's it, relax."

Heather continued to talk to the stallion, who was still very tense. But gradually he began to relax until, by the fourth time around the ring, he was walking forward on a loose rein. After about fifteen minutes of walking, Chauncy told Heather to get off and put Blackjack back in his stall. "We don't want to overdo it, you know. The best thing to do is go very slowly," he advised.

Heather continued to work Blackjack at the walk for several days, and then decided that they were ready to try trotting. "Good boy, good boy. You did it," she praised him as he broke into a trot.

They trotted around the ring several times and, like with the first attempt at the walk, Blackjack started off very tense but gradually relaxed.

Heather kept him going until she felt him puffing for breath.

"There, that wasn't so bad, was it?" Chauncy asked as Heather walked the horse.

"No, it wasn't too bad."

Heather worked Blackjack at the walk and trot every day. By the end of September, they were both comfortable with the routine. Blackjack had relaxed enough that Heather actually took him out on the trail for a short ride. They walked and trotted through the woods and once, while trotting quickly up a long, gently sloping hill, Blackjack broke into a canter. Heather was surprised that he would do such a thing and that he didn't seem to mind at all. She decided to just let him run, hoping that the experience would make it easier when she asked for a canter in the ring. When they reached the top of the hill, Blackjack slowed to a walk and then stopped as he looked around himself. His neck was once again raised up in the proud Morgan stance and his ears were pricked forward. He snorted. There was a small tree limb that had fallen and was blocking the path. Heather dismounted and tried to push the limb out of the way. When she did so, a small branch broke off. "Will you look at that?" she said as she showed the branch to her horse.

Blackjack's eyes bulged and he jumped back in terror.

"What's the matter, boy? It's just a branch, see?" she said as she tried to bring the branch up to his face. But the horse, terrified, tried to back up further and jerked his head off to the side. "Come on, it's not going to eat you. The way you're reacting you might think it's a..." She paused as she realized why her horse was terror-stricken. "You think it's a crop, don't you? I'm so sorry," she said as she threw the

223

branch down. "Someone really must have hurt you. Don't worry; I'll never use a crop on you."

Blackjack continued to stare at the branch on the ground, though, and Heather wondered what her poor horse could be thinking. Perhaps Mr. Spencer had hit him with a crop every time he did something wrong, or more likely, Mr. Spencer just hit him when the mood struck. Disgusted at the thought, she mounted and turned her horse toward the barn.

The following day, Chauncy announced that it was time to try a canter. Blackjack was now going well at a trot, only occasionally tensing up when asked for the gait. Heather worked the horse until Chauncy instructed, "Okay, whenever you're ready, ask for a canter."

Heather was eager to see what his canter was like and was not worried, since she was going to ask for his left lead first. They'd begin with his good lead. "Canter, boy, canter," she ordered, tapping him with her outside leg and pulling back slightly on the outside rein.

But she was not ready for the violent reaction that she got. As soon as Blackjack felt the outside leg on him, he exploded. His head went down as his back and hind legs went up in a frantic effort to dismount his rider. Heather felt the end of his tail hit the back of her head as she first went backward and then was flung forwards, over the horse's head. She continued to hold on to the reins as her body quickly met the ground, fanny first. Blackjack stood perfectly still, too terrified to move.

Chauncy came running over to her. "Are you okay?" he asked, obviously very concerned.

"I think so," she responded slowly. "My shoulder hurts."

"Can you get up?"

"Yeah."

Chauncy helped Heather get to her feet, while she felt her right shoulder.

"I must have hit it on something."

"Let me see."

Chauncy looked at her shoulder and then gently rubbed it with both hands. "Does that hurt?"

"No. I'm just a little shaky. I'll be okay."

"I'll put Blackjack away while you sit down and rest." Chauncy started to lead the horse toward the barn.

"No, wait Chauncy. I'm okay, really. Just a little scared. But I need to keep riding him. If I stop now, we'll never get through this. Didn't you tell me that you should never end a lesson on a bad note?" she asked as she brushed herself off. Then she walked over to the horse, took the reins, and mounted. "Now Blackjack, let's do this right. I'm ready for you now!"

Heather walked the horse around the ring a couple of times to get him to relax, but he wasn't cooperating. He knew that the canter was coming up and he didn't like it. He tried to trot but soon discovered that his rider wanted him to walk, so the agitated horse started walking sideways. His ears, although not flat back against his neck, were pinned back enough to show his displeasure. Finally Heather asked for a canter, but this time she was ready. She had tightened her reins and was using her legs to hold on. Blackjack once again exploded in a violent buck. Heather grabbed a handful of mane and kicked the horse again. "Come on, come on!" she ordered, far more determined to get the horse to canter now.

The horse tried to trot and buck at the same time but his bucking lessened as he continued to trot.

"That's it Heather! Just keep him going. He can't buck if he's moving forward."

By now the horse was moving out in a fast trot. Heather continued to ask for a canter until the horse, unable to go any faster in a trot, broke into a canter.

"Keep him going!" shouted Chauncy.

Blackjack cantered around the ring several times, tossing his head and swishing his tail in annoyance the whole time. At one point she could feel him slowing down, as though he wanted to walk, but she squeezed with her legs and he sped up. Finally satisfied that her horse knew what was expected of him, Heather brought him back down to a walk. "Good boy, good boy," she said as she patted his neck.

The horse was puffing and his neck was wet with sweat—mostly from nerves, not from the actual exertion of the work.

"You did it!" Chauncy praised as he walked over to them. "That was really something!"

"Thanks, Chauncy. I knew we could do it!"

After the horse was cooled down and put away, Chauncy took another look at Heather's shoulder.

"It doesn't feel too bad now. I think I just hit it on Blackjack's head as I flew over him. I'll be okay."

The following day, Heather was at the barn as usual. Her shoulder was a bit stiff, but otherwise she felt fine. She got Blackjack ready and met Chauncy out in the ring, ready to go. After warming the horse up she said, "Okay, Chauncy, I'm ready to try cantering again."

"Okay, but this time let's do it differently. Instead of asking him for a canter, ask for a trot like you did when you first rode him in the spring. And then just keep asking him to go faster. Eventually he'll have to break into a canter. When he does, praise him and then make sure you keep him in it."

"Okay."

Heather asked Blackjack for a trot, something they had just finished doing. The horse obediently broke into a trot, ears forward, and eager to please.

After they had gone around the ring once in a quiet, easy trot, Heather asked her horse to go faster. He sped up and continued to increase his speed until they were trotting so fast that Heather had trouble posting to it.

"How fast can this guy trot?" she hollered.

"Keep going, ask for more speed."

Heather squeezed with both legs and clucked to Blackjack. Finally, unable to go any faster at a trot, the horse broke into a canter.

"Good boy, good boy," she praised him. Blackjack seemed to be unconcerned with the fact that he was cantering, since his ears were still forward and he wasn't tossing his head.

"That was great!" Heather announced to Chauncy as she came back to a walk.

"That's what you need to do then, until he gets over his fear of cantering. Let him get his breath and then try cantering the other way."

That other way was to the right, which was the direction Blackjack hated. But when they trotted first, the horse seemed to forget his problems and, after trotting at top speed, broke into a canter on the right lead without bucking or causing a fuss.

"Good boy," praised Heather once again. "You did it!"

For the next few weeks, Heather continued to work Blackjack in the same way. Before long he was eagerly anticipating the fast trots and each day he was able to go just a little bit faster. Once in the canter, however, Heather began to slow him down until, by the end of the second week, he was doing a nice, slow, rocking horse type of canter. While brushing Blackjack after a particularly good work-out, Heather told Chauncy, "I want to go to the horse show."

"What show?" he asked.

"The Fall Finale Show. Laura told me about it a long time ago."

"You really want to show him?"

"Yes, I do. I think I need to prove to myself that I can do it. He's going well and the show isn't for a few more weeks. We can do it."

"Are you forgetting that you'll have to canter from a walk?"

"No, but I think if I start asking for a canter and not letting him trot so much we'll be okay. I've seen people let their horses trot several steps before can-tering and still place really well. Besides, I'm not going to the show to win some big championship. I just want to see if we can do it."

"Well, that's up to you and your parents. If you feel ready for it then I'll be glad to help you."

"You don't have to. I kinda talked to Laura last week. She's coming home that weekend to help me. Surprise!" Heather said with a sneaky expression.

"You mean my daughter is coming home and she didn't even tell me?"

"Yup, she'll be here, so all you'll have to do is come watch us."

The two weeks before the show went by much too fast. Fall was in full swing but Heather hardly had time to notice. Between working Blackjack and getting all her schoolwork done, she was very busy. Blackjack had improved to the point where he would pick up a canter after several strides at the trot instead of the two times around the ring that it had originally required. And he was starting to relax much more. The tail swishing was gone, as were the pinned back ears, although Heather could still feel him tense up just a bit when she asked for a canter.

The day before the show, Laura arrived home in time to watch Heather work her horse. "He looks great!" she said as she walked up to the ring to watch them.

"Isn't he doing well?" Heather asked, proud of her horse.

"I'd say! You both look great!"

Laura continued to watch the pair as they picked up a canter after only a few strides of trotting. "Wow, how'd you get him to do that?" she asked after Heather had finished working the horse.

"It wasn't easy, but your dad showed me how."

"Are you all set for tomorrow?"

"I think so."

The following morning, Heather and Laura put the finishing touches on the stallion and then loaded him into the trailer. The ride to the show was uneventful, and they arrived in plenty of time.

The show was a small, all breed affair, with a few professional trainers scattered among the exhibitors. The tension that Heather had felt at the big Morgan show was not evident, since most people were just there to have a good time. The air was cool and the horses frisky, their winter coats well started.

The two companions found a vacant stall for Blackjack and then Laura groomed him while Heather got herself ready. Unlike the time she wore it at the Morgan show and almost passed out from the heat, the heavy wool saddle suit felt wonderful in the chilly fall air.

"That looks much better on you than it did on me," Laura laughed as she looked at Heather, all dressed up. "Come on, it's almost time for your class."

"Wow, he looks great!" Heather exclaimed as she looked at her horse. "In fact, he looks just as good as he did at the Morgan show."

"Let's hope the judge thinks so! Come on, let's get to the ring."

Heather and Blackjack silently followed Laura. Waiting outside the ring for their class, Heather got the distinct feeling that somebody was watching her. Turning, she was upset to see Mr. Spencer and another man staring at her. They were too far away for Heather to hear their conversation, but she saw Mr. Spencer say something to his companion as he pointed to Heather and her horse, then laugh and walk away. His friend followed along.

"Did you see that?" she whispered to Laura.

"What?"

"Over there, look quick," Heather said as she pointed.

"Oh geeze, just what we need," Laura groaned.

"What's he doing here?"

"Who knows," Laura replied. "And you know what? Who cares! He's a jerk, don't let him bother you."

"You're right, but it's hard to ignore a man like that."

"Well hey there, kiddo!" came Mr. Richardson's voice.

Heather spun around and saw her parents and the Campbells walking toward her.

"Dad! You made it!"

"Of course I did. You don't think I'd miss this, do you?"

"I'm so happy you could come. You'll never guess who I just saw!"

"Who?" Chauncy asked.

"Mr. Spencer. He was staring at me."

"Don't worry about him," Mrs. Richardson said. "We're here now, and we're not going to let someone like that ruin our fun, are we?"

"Chauncy, he really looks wonderful," Mrs. Campbell commented.

"He sure does. I'm really proud of you, Heather."

Just then, the announcer called her class. "Remember," Chauncy continued, "it doesn't matter how you do, just that you do it!"

Heather smiled, picked up her reins, and made her entrance. Her cheering section made its way to the rail right by the gate. Heather was the first one to enter the ring, and the judge, who was standing in the middle, watched her carefully. Blackjack had his ears forward and was carrying himself in the proud Morgan fashion to which he was accustomed. His neck was raised and flexed at the poll, while his legs went so high that his knees came up almost to the height of his chest. The next horse didn't enter until Heather was almost all the way around the ring. The judge had been watching her the whole time, but when the third horse entered, he turned his attention to the other competitors.

"He likes you!" Chauncy encouraged from the rail.

Two more horses entered the ring, and then the gate was shut.

Only five horses, Heather thought as she continued to trot. *That's good, it will give us plenty of space.*

"Class is in order, all trot please, all trot."

Hearing the announcer made Blackjack raise his legs even higher. He kept his ears forward except for the brief moments when his rider would say something to him. He'd quickly flick one of his ears back to listen and then, once she was finished, he'd return his ear to its forward position.

"Walk please, all walk."

Blackjack slowed to a walk and then tossed his head slightly. He knew that the canter was next and he was starting to feel tense.

"Not now, boy," his rider quietly implored.

"Canter please, canter."

As Heather asked for the canter she looked up to see Mr. Spencer standing by the rail with his friend. He was glaring at her, and it made her nervous. But Blackjack just trotted for several strides and then broke into an easy, relaxed canter. Heather glanced at the judge, but his attention was on the other side of the ring.

"Good boy, good boy, you did it," she encouraged.

"Come on, kiddo, smile! You look so serious!" her dad said as she passed him.

Heather laughed and began to relax. She decided she wasn't going to let Mr. Spencer get the best of her; rather, she was going to show him how great her horse was.

"All walk please, and then reverse and continue walking."

Heather slowed Blackjack down to a walk right in front of Mr. Spencer and reversed direction.

"They've drugged him," she heard him say to his companion.

Heather couldn't believe what she was hearing. Unable to train a horse with love and understanding himself, Mr. Spencer was using excuses to explain the good behavior of her horse. She felt her body tense up as she thought of all the things that Mr. Spencer must have done to her horse. Blackjack suddenly threw his head up and Heather realized that, while thinking of Mr. Spencer, she had unconsciously tightened the reins. She quickly loosened them so that Blackjack could relax.

Once everyone was reversed, the announcer again asked for a trot. Blackjack instantly exploded into a powerful, high-trotting gait. He was having fun showing off and Heather took advantage of it. She let him trot on at a brisk pace and encouraged him with her voice and legs. He felt good, and Heather was so proud of him. His long mane blew back toward her hands and he seemed to grow taller as he continued to trot, since with each stride he appeared to be reaching just a little higher with his knees.

"Walk please, all walk."

Heather asked Blackjack to walk, but the horse was reluctant to slow down. He was enjoying the feeling of trotting so high, and didn't want to stop. His rider had to pull on the reins more than she was used to, and in response, Blackjack tossed his head several times.

"I hope the judge didn't see that," she whispered to herself as Blackjack slowed to a walk. But she was too afraid to look in the judge's direction.

She took a deep breath, knowing that all they had to do now was canter—which seemed so simple, but included so many things that could go wrong.

"All canter please, all canter," came the sudden command.

Heather asked for a canter and again, like the first way around the ring, her horse trotted a few strides and then broke into a wonderful, smooth canter. As they made their way down the side of the ring to where Mr. Spencer was standing, Heather was able to catch a glimpse of the judge, whose attention was elsewhere. Knowing that the judge wasn't looking, Heather looked Mr. Spencer straight in the face and stuck her tongue out. Then she smiled and turned her full attention back to her horse.

"That felt good, didn't it?" she asked her horse quietly.

"Way to go!" Laura laughed as Heather cantered by.

Heather smiled again as she enjoyed the last canter around the ring. Then the announcer asked everyone to walk, and finally to line up in the center of the ring. All five horses walked into the center, where the judge got one last look at them.

After the judge had looked at each horse, he handed his pad of paper to the ringmaster and then left the ring while the ribbons were awarded.

"We have the results of our English Pleasure class," boomed the voice from the speaker.

Heather felt her heart race as she waited. She knew that her goal had been to just have a good ride, and she had. But a blue ribbon would be nice, too! She tried to calm down as she patted her horse.

"The winner of our class is number 23, Gallant Image, owned and ridden by Heather Richardson."

Heather could hear her parents scream in delight as she bent down to hug her horse. "We did it Blackjack! We did it!"

She managed to get out of the barn without setting off the alarm. Someone must have forgotten to set it that night, but she didn't care, she just wanted to get out of there. She jumped onto her horse and walked him quietly past the house. Once they were beyond all the buildings, she asked her horse to canter. He picked up his right lead without a moment's hesitation and cantered gently, careful not to lose his rider. The two of them were soon out of sight, headed down the road toward the morning sun.

The Horse Behind the Books - Blackjack
Registered Name: Rum Brook Immortal Star
(Immortal Command x Rum Brook Athena)
Photo taken at "BreyerFest"
- Courtesy Breyer Animal Creations
Photo by Jennifer Munson